STRAWBERRY HILL

Strawberry Hill

by

Mary Ann Hoberman

illustrated by

Wendy Anderson Halperin

LITTLE, BROWN AND COMPANY
New York Boston

Special thanks to
Anne Rockwell for her encouragement.

Little, Brown and Company

Hachette Book Group
237 Park Avenue, New York, NY 10017
Visit our website at www.lb-kids.com

Little, Brown and Company is a division of Hachette Book Group, Inc.
The Little, Brown name and logo are trademarks of Hachette Book Group, Inc.

First Paperback Edition: May 2010
First published in hardcover in July 2009 by Little, Brown and Company

Hoberman, Mary Ann.
Strawberry Hill / by Mary Ann Hoberman.—1st ed.
p. cm.
Summary: Ten-year-old Allie's family moves from urban New Haven to rural Stamford, Connecticut, in the midst of the Great Depression.
ISBN 978-0-316-04136-2 (hc) / ISBN 978-0-316-04135-5 (pb)
[1. Moving, Household—Fiction. 2. Country life—Fiction. 3. Best friends—Fiction. 4. Friendship—Fiction. 5. Depressions—1929—Fiction. 6. Jews—United States—Fiction.] I. Title.
PZ7.H6525St 2009
[Fic]—dc22
2008045300

10 9 8 7 6 5 4 3 2 1

Book design by Saho Fujii

RRD-C

Printed in the United States of America

To Joel

Beloved little brother

chapter one

You would have thought it was the best news in the world.

"Guess what?" my mother said with a big smile on her face, hanging up the phone. "Daddy's found us a house to rent in Stamford!"

"Just think!" she went on when I didn't say anything. "You'll be able to have your own room and Daddy will live with us all the time! Isn't that wonderful?"

Right now my father only lived with us on weekends. That was because we lived in New Haven and he worked in Stamford, which was too far away to come home from every night. So he lived in the Roger Smith Hotel during the week. It was the Depression, which meant jobs were very hard to get. So when he lost his old job in New Haven and found a new job in Stamford, he had to take it. He said he was really lucky, because lots of fathers didn't have any jobs at all.

"I don't want to move," I said.

"You don't want to have your own room and your own yard and have Daddy live with us all the time?" she asked.

"I like it here," I said. "Besides, I'm the only one that plays in the yard anyway, except for Danny and Ruthie." Danny was my little brother. Ruthie Greenberg lived upstairs and was my best friend. Her parents owned our house.

I knew my mother didn't like living in the Greenbergs' house as much as I did. She was always complaining that our apartment was too small and that it was noisy. And she said Mrs. Greenberg didn't keep her apartment clean enough. My mother kept ours really clean. Mrs. Greenberg told me once that you could eat off our kitchen floor.

"You can eat off mine, too," she said, laughing. "There's certainly enough food there!"

Mrs. Greenberg was really funny. And besides, it was true. But that was because everybody was always sitting around her kitchen table, drinking tea and eating sponge cake and cracking nuts and talking, so lots of crumbs and shells would fall on the floor.

I loved the Greenbergs. They were a big family. Besides Ruthie, who was the youngest and the only girl, there were four big brothers. My favorite was Sidney. He was always telling me new knock-knock jokes, which I would tell everybody at school.

When my father came home on Friday night, my mother gave him a big hug.

"What do you think, Allie?" he asked. "Aren't you looking forward to having your own room?"

"I guess so," I said. Actually, I didn't mind very much sleeping with Danny. We had a great big bed and sometimes when he woke up at night I would make up stories for him.

"You don't sound very enthusiastic," my father said.

"She doesn't want to leave the Greenbergs," my mother said, sounding annoyed. She didn't like it when I spent too much time upstairs. She thought Ruthie was a bad influence on me because sometimes she used swear words that her brothers had taught her.

"What if I don't like my new school?" I asked.

"Of course you'll like it," my father said.

How did he know, I thought. He'd never even seen it.

"What about the house?" Danny asked.

My father told us that it had six rooms and two bathrooms and a cellar and an attic and a garage and a screened-in back porch and a big backyard. And there was a brick fireplace in the living room.

"Can we toast marshmallows?" Danny asked in an excited voice.

"I don't see why not," my father said. "And there's another

good thing," he added. "Our street's a dead end so there's hardly any traffic."

"What's at the end of it?" I asked.

"A great big field."

I asked him the name of the street.

"Strawberry Hill," my father said. "Our new address is 12 Strawberry Hill."

chapter *two*

Strawberry Hill! I was going to live on a street called Strawberry Hill! All of a sudden I didn't mind moving so much after all.

I could picture it perfectly. It was a wide grassy slope that you could roll down and then come to a stop at a beautiful stone wall you could walk on, with a little gate you could go through just like Alice in Wonderland. And all over the hill there were strawberries, big fat red juicy strawberries, and you could pick as many as you wanted because they were growing on your street so they were yours.

It was the middle of May and we were going to move at the end of June, as soon as school was over. I made a calendar to mark off the days. For moving day I drew a great big strawberry.

"You seem happy you're moving," Ruthie said when she saw it. "I thought you liked living here."

"I do," I said. "You know I do."

We went upstairs to her kitchen. Mrs. Greenberg was at the stove. When she saw me, she gave me a hug. She smelled like cooking.

"So you'll be leaving us soon," she said. "We're all going to miss you."

"I'll miss you, too," I said. Even after knowing about Strawberry Hill, it was still sad to think about not living with the Greenbergs.

"Well, maybe you can come back to visit us," she said.

"We can write to each other," Ruthie said.

"That's a good idea," said Mrs. Greenberg. "And I'll make you a surprise and send it to you in the mail so you won't forget us."

I told her I'd never forget them. I wondered what kind of surprise she would make for me. She was really good at sewing. She always made Ruthie's dresses and she'd helped my mother make our kitchen curtains. They were green and white checks with red zigzag trim.

My mother decided not to take them to our new house.

"But they're so pretty," I said. "They'd be like a souvenir."

"They probably wouldn't fit the windows. Anyway, I want fresh ones. I'll leave these here for the next tenants."

The Greenbergs had already rented our apartment again, to a family with a little girl. They were going to move in the week after we left, after Mr. Greenberg and the boys had painted all the rooms. Danny's and my room was going to be pink, they said.

"Can my room on Strawberry Hill be pink?" I asked my mother. It was blue, Daddy had said. Blue was for boys.

"We're not painting anything," she said. "The whole house was repainted last year."

I went to ask my father. "What did your mother just tell you?" he said.

"But Mr. Greenberg says they always paint the rooms again when somebody new moves in. So why don't we?"

"What did I just tell you?" he asked.

"I could do it myself," I said. "If you bought me some pink paint and a brush, I could paint it myself."

My father laughed. Then he shook his head. "Sorry," he said. "Money . . ."

I finished for him. ". . . doesn't grow on trees."

We both laughed. It was what my mother always said, only when she said it, she wasn't joking. When my father and I said it, we were. But we never said it when she was around. It seemed like my mother was always worrying about money, about how expensive everything was and how we couldn't afford to buy things. Sometimes when my father brought back a present for us from Stamford, instead of being happy, she got mad at him. Mr. and Mrs. Greenberg never got mad at each other.

chapter three

"It's here!" Danny yelled.

He had been standing by the kitchen window all morning, watching for the moving truck. Now it was finally here. It was a huge green truck with MOLLY'S MOVING painted on the side. I wondered who Molly was.

Three moving men came in and my father started showing them what to take. They weren't taking our bed, Danny's and mine, because in our new house we were each going to have a brand-new bed, just big enough for one person. Mr. Greenberg was going to sell it for us. And there were a few other things we were leaving behind, like the kitchen table, which had a wobbly leg and really belonged to the Greenbergs anyway.

My mother and I had already packed all of our dishes, our everyday ones and the good ones that we never used except for company. I had wrapped each separate piece in newspaper and my mother had packed them all into the cardboard boxes we had gotten from the grocery store. I was especially careful with the three teacups my grandmother had brought over with her from Russia a long time ago. Once there had been twelve of them, my mother told me, but all the others had broken. They were made out of porcelain and they were so thin that the light shone through them. And they had borders of tiny pink roses and rims of gold that were almost worn away.

After the moving men left, we loaded up our car with the things we were taking with us: a picnic lunch, some other bags of food, and a few boxes packed with special things. Two of them were mine. One had my dolls. The other had all my books and the special folders I had made out of my father's shirt cardboards where I kept all my stories and poems.

Then we all went back into the house to make sure we hadn't forgotten anything. The empty rooms looked sad with no furniture or pictures. I went into our bedroom by myself. Over in a corner, where our bureau had been, I saw the copper bracelet with the two turquoise stones that my Aunt Sadie had brought back for me from Arizona last summer and that I thought I had lost. It was all dusty. I blew it off and put it in my pocket.

"Good-bye, room," I whispered. I tried to imagine how it would look when it was painted pink with someone else living in it. I wondered if she would get to be friends with the Greenbergs and if they would like her better than me.

"Time to go," my mother called from the kitchen.

When we went out to the porch, Mrs. Greenberg and Ruthie were standing there waiting to say good-bye. The night before we had all gone upstairs and had supper with them.

Mrs. Greenberg hugged me and Danny. Then she hugged my mother, but just a little.

"Sam and the boys say good-bye," she said. It was a weekday so they were all working at the store. "We all wish you luck in your new home."

"Thank you for everything," my father said, shaking hands with her.

"I'll write to you," I said to Ruthie.

My father got in the car and started the motor. "Next stop, Stamford!" he yelled. "All aboard!"

My mother and Danny got in. I started to follow them and then turned back. I took the bracelet out of my pocket. Without saying anything, I put it in Ruthie's hand.

"Hurry up, Allie!" my mother called.

I ran down the path, got into the car, and we drove away. When I looked back, Mrs. Greenberg and Ruthie were still on the porch, waving good-bye.

chapter four

With the four of us in the car, plus all the boxes and bags, we could hardly move. My mother and Danny were in the back as usual and my father and I were in the front. I always sat in the front because I got carsick.

The trouble was, my father smoked, which made me feel like throwing up. Usually I'd let him know in time and he would pull over to the side of the road and let me out. But sometimes I couldn't hold it in and then it was awful. Throw-up would splash all over and we'd have to stop and my mother would wipe me off with the towel she always had with her and the car would be smelly and I would be, too.

But my mother never got mad at me for throwing up, she just got mad at my father.

"Do you have to smoke in the car?" she would ask him. "You know it makes Allie nauseous."

But my father wouldn't stop. He smoked almost all the time, even in bed. The cigarettes he smoked were called Lucky Strikes and they came in a green package. He smoked two or three packages a day.

I was glad it wasn't raining today so we could open the car windows. When I stuck my head out the window and felt the breeze and breathed in the fresh air, I usually was all right. And if we played a game, that helped, too.

Today we were counting license plates to see how many different states we could find. By the time we were in Bridgeport and ready to stop and have lunch, we had found seven: Connecticut, Massachusetts, New York, New Jersey, Rhode Island, Vermont, and Wyoming. We had never seen a Wyoming before.

We pulled up at a gas station. The gasoline man washed our windows and gave Danny and me lollipops, red for him and green for me. We couldn't pick our colors and Danny wouldn't trade. I hated green.

"Never mind," said my mother. "You can't have it now anyway. It will spoil your appetite."

The gas station had a picnic table outside and we ate our lunch there. When we finished and got back in the car, Danny fell asleep on my mother's lap so we couldn't turn on the radio.

"How much longer?" I asked.

"About an hour," my father said. "We'll get there around three o'clock."

The car clock said three minutes after two. I looked out the window.

"Where are we now?"

"This is Fairfield."

"Is Fairfield close to Stamford?"

"About an hour away."

"You said that before."

"Five minutes ago. Just be patient."

I looked at the car clock again. The big hand had hardly moved. I closed my eyes and started to think about Strawberry Hill. I wondered how big the strawberries would be and whether there were enough for everybody on the street. I wondered how they stopped robbers from coming at night and stealing them. Was there a fence? Maybe the fathers took turns staying up all night and guarding them.

My father lit a new cigarette from his old one. I began to cough.

"Just a little while longer," my mother said. "Breathe in some fresh air."

I looked at the clock. "Forty-four," I said. "We still have forty-four minutes."

I swallowed hard and took a lick of my green lollipop. Even though I felt sick, I didn't want to stop driving. I shut my eyes again and pretended I was at the top of Strawberry Hill, ready to roll to the bottom. I stretched out my arms and legs and began to turn over and over in the soft green grass, picking big red strawberries on the way down.

"Here we are!"

My father's voice jolted me awake. I opened my eyes. We were parked in the driveway of a white house with green shutters. I got out of the car and ran back to the sidewalk. All I saw was a street with houses on either side. It didn't look much different from New Haven.

"Well, what do you think?" my father asked, smiling. "What do you think of our new house?"

"But this isn't Strawberry Hill," I said. "You said we were going to live on Strawberry Hill."

"Of course it is," he answered.

"But . . ." I looked all around again. "Where are the strawberries?"

"Don't be silly," my mother said. "Strawberry Hill is just the name of the street. That doesn't mean there are strawberries growing on it."

"Then why did they call it that?"

"How should I know?" my mother said, starting to take things out of the car. "Maybe someone just liked the name. Now stop complaining and help us carry some bags inside. Don't you want to see your room?"

I picked up the bag with my dolls in it. I had promised them that as soon as we got here I would spread one of their blankets on the grass and we would all have a strawberry party together.

As I followed my mother up the front path, I saw someone standing in the yard next door staring at us.

"Who's that?" I asked my father.

"That must be one of the Bryant girls," he said. "The Bryants live next door. They seem very nice."

I wondered if we'd be friends and if we'd be in the same grade and if we would walk to school together. And I wondered if she had ever wondered why there were no strawberries on Strawberry Hill.

chapter five

The house was almost empty. The moving men weren't going to deliver our furniture until later. In the living room was a brand-new couch my parents had bought. It was a purply velvet and my mother said we couldn't sit on it in our play clothes. In the dining room there was a beautiful new table and six chairs made out of dark shiny wood. We hadn't had a dining room in New Haven.

"Is this where we'll eat?" I asked.

"Only on special occasions," my mother said.

Danny asked her what a special occasion was and she said holidays and when we had company.

"Are birthdays special occasions?" I asked.

"They are," my mother said, "but I don't know if we'll use the dining room for them. They get very messy."

We went into the kitchen. It was bigger than the one in New Haven.

"Isn't this beautiful?" my mother asked. She put the bags on the counter. "I've always wanted a nice kitchen."

"I liked the old one," I said.

"Where's my room?" Danny asked.

I had almost forgotten about my new room. We followed my mother upstairs. It felt funny having a stairway inside your own house. At the top of the stairs was a hall with four doors. They were all closed. One of them opened and my father came out of the bathroom.

Danny was jumping up and down. "Which one is my room?"

My father opened the door next to the bathroom and we all went in. It was pretty small compared to our old room and it had only one window. The walls had green and white striped wallpaper on them. Danny started racing around in circles. My father told him to calm down, but he was smiling. I could tell he was glad that Danny was so excited about his new room.

Then my father looked at me. "Don't you want to see your new room, Allie?"

I shrugged. "I don't care."

"What's the matter with her?" my father asked my mother.

"She's disappointed because there are no strawberries on Strawberry Hill," my mother said, laughing. "Can you imagine?"

I felt my face getting hot.

"I hate you!" I screamed. "I hate you and I hate this house and I wish we had never moved!"

I ran out of Danny's room, down the stairs, and out the front door, slamming it behind me. When I got to the sidewalk, I stopped and looked around. The street was empty and quiet. Beginning at our house it sloped a little toward the end. So it was a sort of hill after all, even if it wasn't a very big one. And at the bottom there was a stone wall, just as I had imagined. And in the wall, at the end of the sidewalk — I squinched my eyes to make sure — there was a white gate!

I started to run down the hill, past the houses after ours. There were three of them. The one next door to us was made out of bricks. It was smaller than our house, only one story high. The next one was gray stone with a pointy roof that made it look a little like a castle. The last house, just before the gate, was wood like ours, only yellow with a big front porch.

And then I was at the gate in the wall. I lifted up the rusty handle and it swung open. On the other side of the wall there was a big field full of weeds and bushes.

"Watch out!"

I turned around. A girl was standing behind me, the one I had seen when we first arrived.

"Watch out for what?" I asked.

"Look at your shoe."

I looked down. One of my shoes was right next to a circle of brown glop. When I pulled it away, some of the glop stuck to the side. It looked sort of like dog doo but it was really big.

"What is it?" I asked her.

"Don't you know?"

Scraping my shoe over the ground to get the stuff off, I shook my head.

"It's a cow plop," she said. "You know, number two from a cow."

"But how did it get here?"

She pointed. And there, over at the other side of the field, were two cows! Real cows, brown with white spots and horns.

"Mooo!" the girl called in a loud voice.

"Mooo," a cow mooed back.

"Are they yours?" I asked.

She laughed. "Of course not. They belong to Mr. Sherwood. He owns the farm."

"What farm?"

"This one, silly! Where we are now."

"This is a farm?" I had never been on a farm before, but this just looked like an old field.

"It's a little one. Just this field and the apple orchard and the barn over there." She pointed to a red building behind the cows. "But Mr. Sherwood is a real farmer. He owns two cows and a pony and some sheep and some pigs and lots of chickens. And sometimes he lets us help him milk the cows or pick apples. And sometimes he gives us a ride in the pony cart."

I couldn't believe it. We had moved almost next door to a farm with cows and a pony and pigs and sheep and chickens and no one had even told me about it. As if it wasn't even important. Or maybe they didn't know. Suddenly I remembered why I was here and what I had yelled before I'd run out of the house.

"I better go home," I said.

"My name is Martha," the girl said. "I live next door to you."

"I'm Allie," I said. "What grade are you in?"

"I'm going into fourth."

"I am, too," I said. "Maybe we'll be in the same class."

"Are you Catholic?"

I shook my head.

"Then we won't be in the same school. I go to parochial school."

"What's that?" I asked.

"It's where Catholics go," she said. "What are you?"

"I'm Jewish," I answered.

"Then you'll probably go to Center School and be in the same class with Mimi Minnick. Poor you."

"Why poor me?"

As we talked, we started walking back across the field and through the gate.

"Because she's a crybaby. She lives over there." Martha pointed across the street to a green house with a big front yard. "They hardly ever mow the grass."

"I wish I could go to school with you instead of Mimi Minnick," I said.

"Well, you can't," Martha said. "But when school starts, we can still play together in the afternoons."

By now we were in front of my house. The big moving truck was in the driveway and the moving men were unloading it.

"If you want, I'll come call for you tomorrow morning after breakfast," Martha said.

"Okay," I said. I looked down at my shoe to make sure all the cow plop was gone. Then I went inside.

chapter six

In the front hall my mother was telling the moving men where to put things. When she saw me, she looked angry for a minute. Then all of a sudden she smiled.

"Let's forget about what happened," she said. "We were both upset. Go up and see your room."

I went upstairs. Danny was in his room unpacking his box of toys.

"That's your room," he said, pointing across the hall. "It's not fair. It's bigger than mine."

"Well, I'm bigger than you are, too," I said.

The door was shut. When I opened it, I started to laugh.

It was pink!

The whole room was pink, even the ceiling!

And right in the middle there was a brand new bed and it was pink, too!

I closed my eyes and opened them again.

Everything was still pink.

I ran downstairs and threw my arms around my mother.

"I'm sorry!" I said. "I don't hate you! I'll never say I hate you again!"

"You can thank Daddy," she said. "It was his idea."

"Do you like it?" he asked.

"I love it more than anything in the whole world!"

"Daddy painted it himself," my mother said.

"Maybe that will make up for the strawberries," he said. "What do you think?"

I had forgotten all about the strawberries. I nodded. Then I told them about the farm.

"A farm?" my mother asked. "Are you sure?"

"Martha told me," I said. All of a sudden I remembered. "Look!" I lifted up my foot and stuck out the edge of my shoe. "Cow plop. It's all gone but you can smell it."

My father sniffed. "Cow plop, sure enough," he said. "I thought I heard some mooing the other day. Well, that's another bonus, isn't it?"

"Who's Martha?" my mother asked.

"She lives next door," I said. "She's going to call for me tomorrow morning."

"So you've already made a friend," my father said. "That's nice."

I ran back to my room. By now there were some boxes there and the bureau from our old bedroom. My mother came in with scissors and opened up the boxes.

"You can start putting away your clothes," she said.

Now that I had the whole bureau to myself, there was lots of room for everything. I put my underwear in one of the top drawers and my socks and hankies in the other. The middle one was for blouses and shirts and the bottom one for play-suits and shorts and sweaters.

"That's a good job," my mother said. "Now try to keep it all nice and neat."

She was hanging up my dresses and skirts in the closet. They hardly took up half the space. I took my party shoes and slippers and everyday shoes and arranged them on the closet floor.

"What about my toys?"

"Put them on the floor for now. Your father will build you some shelves as soon as he has time."

I got the box with my dolls in it and started taking them out. At our old house they had lived in a bookcase under the window that I had pretended was a dollhouse, but it was attached to the wall and we couldn't take it with us. I had five dolls: Elsie, Oliver, Clara, Shirley (for Shirley Temple), and Honeybunch. Oliver and Elsie were twins. They each wore sailor suits, except Elsie's had a skirt. Honeybunch was a Dy-Dee Doll who wet her diapers when you gave her a bottle. She was my favorite. I had another doll my grandfather had sent me for my last birthday, but I hardly ever played with her because she was too fancy. She had lived in a box on my mother's closet shelf.

I asked my mother if she had remembered to take her.

She nodded. "Would you like to have her stay in your new room?"

"Oh, yes!"

"You'll have to take good care of her."

I promised I would. My mother went and got the big white box she was kept in. I decided that would be her bed for now. I lifted the cover and there she was, all wrapped in tissue paper.

When my mother left, I apologized to my dolls about the strawberry party and told them not to be jealous of Grandpa's doll, even though she was so fancy and had such pretty clothes. I decided to name her Jane.

"Besides, you can all sleep with me in my new bed tonight," I told them. "Jane has to sleep in her box so she won't get wrinkled."

I arranged them all on the bed against the pillow and

looked around my room. Everything looked perfect except our old scratched-up bureau. It was the only thing that wasn't pink. I decided that as soon as we were settled, I would ask if I could paint that pink, too. A darker kind of pink. The color of strawberries.

chapter *seven*

The next morning while I was eating breakfast Martha came to call for me. She stood in our backyard and yelled, "Allie! Hey, Allie!"

I had never had anybody call for me before. In New Haven whenever Ruthie wanted to play, she just came downstairs and knocked at the door.

"Finish your cereal," my mother said.

I was eating oatmeal in my Shirley Temple bowl. It was blue and had her picture on the bottom. I liked to see Shirley Temple, but I hated oatmeal. I ate a few spoonfuls, then drank some milk to take away the taste. I pushed the oatmeal to the side so I could see Shirley Temple's face in the middle.

"Eat some more," my mother said. "Don't you want to grow up to be big and strong?"

I took another spoonful and gulped down the rest of my milk. Then, before my mother could say anything, I ran out the door.

Martha was waiting in the driveway. We each said hi and then just stood there looking at each other.

"What do you want to do?" she asked finally.

"I don't know," I said. "What do you?"

"I don't know either," she answered. "Do you like to jump rope?"

"Sometimes. We need another person though."

"Not if we tie one end to the garage door."

"I only have a regular jump rope," I said. "It isn't long enough."

"I have some clothesline," she said. "Do you want to play in your yard or mine?"

"I don't care."

"Well, let's play in mine then. Mine is nicer."

I followed her through a small opening in the tall prickly hedge that divided our backyards. Even though I knew it wasn't polite to brag, her yard really was nicer than ours. It had a garden at the back with all sorts of pretty flowers, pink and yellow and purple. And there was a swing set and a picnic table and even a statue. It was a man with a beard, wearing a long dress and holding a bird on his arm.

"Who's that?" I asked.

"St. Francis."

"Who's he?"

"He's a saint who loved birds and animals."

"What's a saint?" I asked her.

Martha looked at me like I was crazy. "You don't know what a saint is?"

I shook my head.

"Saints are really holy," she said. "They can do miracles. You pray to them."

"Like praying to God?" I asked.

"I pray to our Holy Father and our Lord Jesus Christ."

"I only pray to God," I said. I was really shocked. I had always thought that Jesus and Christ were swear words. The only time I had ever heard them before was when my father got really mad.

"Do you know Teddy Bear?" Martha asked.

I nodded. We went into her garage to get the rope. When we came out, she tied one end to the garage door handle.

"You can go first," she said.

Martha began to turn the rope and I started to jump while we both chanted.

Teddy Bear, Teddy Bear, go upstairs
Teddy Bear, Teddy Bear, say your prayers

Teddy Bear, Teddy Bear, turn off the light
Teddy Bear, Teddy Bear, say good night
One, two, three, four, five . . .

I missed on six and Martha handed the end of the rope to me. We started again and she got all the way to seventeen before she missed.

"You're good," I said.

"I know," she answered. "I'm even better than my sister and she's ten."

"You have a sister?"

"Claire. We're both named after saints."

Saints again.

"I'm named after my great-grandmother," I said. "She's dead."

"You could be named after a saint, too," Martha said.

"I'm not. Only my great-grandmother."

A girl came out of the back door. She was tall and had long blond braids tied with plaid ribbons.

"That's Claire," Martha said.

Claire came over to us and told Martha she had to get ready. Martha introduced us and Claire smiled at me. She was really pretty.

"We're going shopping for new uniforms," she said.

"For school," Martha explained. "At parochial school you

have to wear uniforms."

Claire wrinkled her nose. "They're hideous."

I had never heard of uniforms for school. The only uniforms I knew about were for policemen and firemen and soldiers.

"What do they look like?" I asked.

"Navy blue jumpers and white blouses," Claire said.

"And navy blue kneesocks and black shoes," Martha added.

"They let us wear our own sweaters," Claire said. "But they have to be navy blue. Next year I'm going to Sacred Heart Academy. They wear plaid skirts."

Martha untied the rope and put it away.

"If you want, I'll call for you after lunch," she said.

I nodded and walked back through the prickly hedge opening into our yard. My mother came out onto the back porch.

"Would you please play with your brother for a while?" she said. "He's been waiting for you all morning."

I went into the house and found Danny up in his room. He wanted to play drawing pictures and telling stories. It was our favorite game together. I went and got some paper and a pencil. The way we played was first I would divide the page up into squares, like the Sunday funny papers.

Then I would start drawing people in one square after another, making up stories about them and giving them all kinds of adventures. Sometimes Danny would make up a story and tell me what to draw.

We were still playing when our mother called us for lunch.

chapter eight

When we finished lunch, Danny wanted to play some more but I said I couldn't because I was going to play with Martha. While I waited for her, I sat at the kitchen table, coloring in an old coloring book. There were a few pictures left that weren't colored in yet. When I had finished them all, Martha still hadn't called for me.

"Go out in the backyard and play with Danny," my mother said. "Martha will find you there."

But I didn't want to. Instead I went out the front door and sat down on the stoop. I looked over at Martha's house but I didn't see anybody. She had probably forgotten all about calling for me.

I saw someone in the yard across the street, the yard where Martha said they hardly ever cut the grass. It was a chubby girl, probably the one Martha had told me about who lived there. While I was looking at her, she waved at me. I waved back.

I got up and crossed the street over to where she was standing.

"You're Mimi," I said.

"How do you know?" she asked me.

"Martha told me."

"You know Martha already?" she said. "You just moved in."

"I met her yesterday," I said. "Down the hill at the farm. We jumped rope this morning in her yard."

Mimi stared at me. "You jumped rope with Martha?"

"She's really good," I said. "She got to twenty-two in Teddy Bear."

"I've never jumped rope with Martha," Mimi said. "I've never even been in her yard."

I remembered what Martha had said about Mimi being a crybaby. She looked as if she was about to cry right now.

"Martha says we go to the same school. What grade are you in?"

Mimi looked sort of embarrassed. "I was in the third grade last year," she said.

"Then maybe we'll be in the same class," I said. "I'm going into fourth grade, too."

Once again Mimi looked as if she wanted to cry. "I'm still in third grade," she said. "I stayed back."

I asked her why.

"I was absent a lot," she explained. "And I'm not a very good reader."

"You'll get better," I said. "My best friend Ruthie in New Haven didn't learn how to read until she was almost eight."

"I'm nine," Mimi said.

"I'm thirsty," I said. "I'd better go home."

"You can come in my house and get a drink," Mimi said. "Soda."

"Soda?" We never had soda except for parties. My mother said it rotted your teeth.

"Cherry or orange," Mimi said. "Or cream."

We walked up her driveway. Weeds grew up in the gravel and scratched our legs. Her backyard was mostly dirt with hardly any grass. In front of the cellar door there was a big pile of coal. The Greenbergs used coal, too, but in our new house we had an oil burner. My mother said it was much cleaner.

We went up the stairs to the back porch. It was full of old furniture pushed against each other, indoor furniture, chairs and tables and a raggedy couch. You could hardly get through it to the back door.

"My father's supposed to take all this stuff to the dump," Mimi said.

She opened the door and I followed her inside into the kitchen. A very fat lady, who I decided must be Mimi's mother, was sitting at the kitchen table, drinking coffee and smoking a cigarette. Hardly any mothers I knew smoked cigarettes, only fathers. My Aunt Florence did but she lived in New York City. On the table there was a big glass ashtray full of cigarette butts.

"This is Allie," Mimi said. "She just moved in across the street."

"Hello, Allie," Mrs. Minnick said. "Welcome to the neighborhood." She coughed.

"We're thirsty," Mimi said. "We came to get some soda."

"That's nice," her mother said. She coughed some more.

Mimi went to the ice box and opened it. "There's cream and cherry," she said. "No orange."

"I'll have cream, please," I said.

"I will, too," said Mrs. Minnick.

Mimi got three jelly glasses from a cupboard. Then she got a bottle opener and pried the bottle top off. She poured the soda very slowly so that the foam didn't overflow.

"Go get some cookies," Mrs. Minnick said.

Mimi opened another cupboard door. The shelves were full of boxes of cookies and crackers all piled up higgledy-piggledy. There were at least twenty boxes of all different kinds. In our house we only had one or two boxes of cookies at a time, which we finished before we bought some more. They lasted a long time, too, because my mother only allowed us two with milk in the afternoon and two after supper.

Mimi brought three boxes to the table. They were all open already.

"Aren't there any chocolate ones?" Mrs. Minnick asked.

"We ate them last night," Mimi said.

Mrs. Minnick stubbed out her cigarette and picked up one of the boxes. It was Lorna Doones.

"Help yourself," she said, taking a handful herself and then giving me the box. I took one out.

"Don't be shy," Mrs. Minnick said. "Take some more." She had already gobbled down her cookies and was getting more out of another box. "I love sweets," she said. "Mimi does, too. She takes after me that way."

Mimi looked embarrassed. She hadn't taken a cookie yet.

"I love Lorna Doones," I said. "They're my favorites."

"Then have some more," Mrs. Minnick said. "Once you open the box, they get stale if you don't eat them right away."

I had already eaten three and had finished my soda. "I think I'd better go home," I said. "My mother doesn't know where I am."

"My, you're a reliable girl," Mrs. Minnick said in a sarcastic voice. "I wish Mimi was as reliable as you are."

I could tell she was making fun of me. She started to cough again.

I got up from the table and pushed my chair in. "Thank you for the soda and cookies," I said.

"Thank you for coming," Mrs. Minnick said. "I'm sure you and Mimi will be really good friends. Say good-bye to your new friend, Mimi."

Mimi mumbled good-bye without looking at me.

When I got home, Martha was standing on our front walk.

"I was looking for you," she said. "Were you playing with Mimi Minnick?"

"Not really. We had soda and cookies."

"I'd never play with her," Martha said. "She smells."

"No, she doesn't," I said.

"Yes, she does," Martha said. "I've smelled her."

"Well, she didn't smell today," I said. "You told me you were going to call for me after lunch."

"No, I didn't."

That was a lie. And she didn't even act sorry about it. When Ruthie couldn't play with me after she promised to, she apologized.

"Anyway," said Martha. "I'm here now. What should we do?"

"I have to go inside," I said.

"Well, if that's the way you feel."

As I went into my house, I felt all mixed up. I didn't really want to be friends with Mimi, but I felt sorry for her. And I did want to be friends with Martha, but I didn't like what she had said about Mimi and how she had lied to me.

All of a sudden I really missed Ruthie. I decided I would go up to my room and write to her now. I had a box of writing paper that I had hardly used any of yet because until now I hadn't had anybody to write to.

I wasn't sure what to write. I sat on my bed for a long time, chewing on my pencil and thinking. Should I tell her about meeting Martha and Mimi? But then, if I did, would I have to tell her about what had just happened? In the end I decided to just write about the farm and the cows and the cow plop and about my new room. At the end of the letter I put a P.S.

And by the way, there aren't any strawberries on our street after all. The name is a lie.

I folded the letter and put it in an envelope and addressed it. Then I went downstairs to ask my mother for a stamp. When she saw that I had written to Ruthie, she asked me if I had told her about my new friend next door.

"Sort of," I answered. I didn't tell her that I wasn't really sure now whether I had a new friend next door or not.

chapter nine

It was Sunday. On Sundays almost everybody else on the street went to church or Sunday School, but there wasn't any Jewish Sunday School in the summer. Earlier I had watched from my bedroom window as Martha and Claire and their parents got into their car to go to mass. Martha said nobody went to heaven except Catholics. When I asked my father what happened to Jews after they died and why we couldn't go to heaven like Catholics, he told me it was hogwash.

"Don't listen to all that hogwash," he said. "Jews go to heaven just like everyone else. We probably even go more because we're the chosen people. But we don't brag about it."

Martha and Claire were wearing hats and white gloves and carrying their white leather catechisms. Mrs. Bryant was wearing a hat, too, a straw one with fake blue flowers that matched her blue dress. Martha said that she changed the flowers on her hat to go with her dress. She had a big box with almost every color flower and lots of green leaves. Martha had shown me. She would twist their stems onto a piece of wire and then she wrapped the wire around her hat. So even though she wore the same hat every Sunday, it always looked different because of the flowers. I wished I could wear a hat like Martha and Claire did, but I didn't have any place to wear one. Even on the High Holy Days, Jewish girls didn't wear hats to Temple. Only boys did.

Martha and I had made up the next day and we had played together all week. But today we wouldn't be able to because on Sundays after church they went over to their grandmother's house for dinner and stayed there all afternoon.

I sat on our front stoop and tried to decide what to do. I spied a big piece of shiny coal I hadn't noticed before over in our driveway. I picked it up and tried it out on the sidewalk. It was perfect. So I started drawing squares for hopscotch. I drew them over the old ones, which you could hardly see anymore. Martha and I had played a few times, but then she didn't want to anymore because Claire said hopscotch was for babies.

I had just finished the squares and was putting in the numbers when Mimi came out of her front door and crossed the street.

"What are you doing?" she asked me.

"What do you think I'm doing?" I said. Even though it wasn't exactly a nice thing to say, I said it in a perfectly nice way.

"Making a hopscotch." She waited until I finished the eight. "Can I play?"

"If you want to," I said. "I wasn't really going to play now. I was just drawing it because I found this good piece of coal." I showed it to her.

"I put it there," she said.

"What?"

"I put it in your driveway. I knew you'd find it."

She was really strange. "You put this piece of coal in my driveway?"

"It's from our coal pile," she said. "I saw you playing hopscotch the other day so I thought you might like it."

"Well, I do," I answered.

"It was a present."

She was really strange. But then when I started thinking about it, even though a piece of coal was a weird kind of present, I had actually liked it almost as much as a real present.

"Maybe if you want, we can play now," I said.

When I said we could play hopscotch, Mimi looked so happy you'd think I had given her a present, too.

Sort of like the present she had given me. Neither of them had cost any money, but we both really liked them. My mother always said that it's the thought that counts about giving gifts, as if it didn't matter what they were only that you were thinking about that person or they were thinking about you. I had always thought that was silly, because of course it's important what kind of present you get. But I could see that Mimi was as happy now as if I'd given her a brand-new toy wrapped up and tied with a ribbon.

We each found a flat stone in my driveway and we did one potato to see who went first. Mimi won. She dropped her stone on the first square, hopped in, picked it up, and hopped out again. She threw her stone into the second square, but it bounced out again and she had to put it back in the first one. I got all the way to seven, where I missed. Mimi picked up her stone and tried again for two. This time her stone stayed there. She hopped in, bent over to pick it up, and lost her balance.

"That's okay," I told her. "Try again."

"But that's not fair," she said. "I'm only supposed to have one turn."

"You probably haven't played for a while," I said. "You're just out of practice."

Mimi was still standing in the second square. "I've never

played hopscotch with anybody before," she said in a whisper. "I've only watched."

"You've never played *hopscotch*?" I asked.

"Just by myself, in my backyard. Where nobody can see me."

We started to play again. By the end of the morning she was pretty good. She could throw her stone so that it didn't bounce when it landed and she almost always got it in the first time up to five. She was still having trouble with six, seven, and eight, but so did most people. I had taught her how to keep her balance on one foot when she picked up her stone by leaning a little to the side as she bent over. She had even tied me one game.

Every time we finished a game, she would beg me to play another one, even though I could see how tired she was getting. Her face was red and she was really sweating. But she didn't want to stop. Finally I said I was tired. She got that crybaby look again and I asked her what was the matter. She told me that she was afraid that if we stopped, I'd never play with her again.

"You're only playing with me today because Martha's at church," she said. "If she was here, you wouldn't."

Of course that was true. At least that was the way it had started. But now I didn't feel that way anymore. Actually I had kind of liked playing with her, teaching her and seeing her get better. And it made her so happy. I told her we could play again tomorrow.

"Not all morning though," I said. "We'll play three games."

"And the day after tomorrow?" she asked. "Can we play then, too?"

I told her we'd see, but she looked so sad that I promised we'd play then, too.

"But that's all," I said. "We might play after that, we probably will, but not every single day. I don't know what I'll be doing every single day. You don't either."

"Yes, I do," she said. "Nothing."

"You have to do something," I said.

"No, I don't," she answered.

"Doesn't your mother make you?"

"No. Does yours?"

"Of course," I said. "She makes me set the table and dry the dishes and play with my brother and make my bed and pick up my room."

"My mother doesn't," Mimi said. "She doesn't make me do any of those things."

"Not even pick up your room?"

She shook her head.

"Well, I have to go in now," I said.

"Should I call for you tomorrow morning?" Mimi asked.

I thought a minute about which would be worse, having Martha see Mimi calling for me, maybe even calling for me at the same time, or having her see me going over to Mimi's house. Finally I told Mimi that I would come and get her. That seemed better.

chapter ten

The next morning I dawdled over my breakfast. I was really sorry I had promised Mimi to come over. It wasn't exactly that I didn't want to play with her, it was more that I didn't want Martha to see me playing with her.

The telephone rang. My mother handed me the receiver.

"Hello," I said.

It was Mimi. Her voice was all choky. She told me that she couldn't play with me this morning because her father was there.

"I really wanted to play hopscotch with you," she said. "I really did."

"I know," I said, trying to sound disappointed. "Well, maybe another time."

"You said tomorrow, remember? You promised we could play tomorrow."

"Well, I'm not so sure now," I said. "I may have to go somewhere."

"But you promised!" She was really crying now. I could tell, even over the telephone.

"All right, Mimi! You don't have to cry about it. I'll play with you tomorrow."

Without waiting for her to answer, I hung up.

So now I didn't have to play with her this morning after all. But somehow I didn't feel as happy about it as I thought I would. I remembered how I felt one time last summer when Sidney was going to take Ruthie and me for a ride to the beach in his car with the rumble seat and I'd looked forward to it all week long and then just as we were leaving, my grandmother came over and my mother said I couldn't go. That was probably how Mimi felt now.

While I was sitting there, chewing on my last bite of toast and looking out the window, Martha came running through the hedge and waved at me. I went outside.

"Guess what?" she said, looking really excited. "Cynthia's back!"

I didn't say anything.

"She's coming over for lunch. Can you come, too?"

We went inside to ask my mother. I already knew about

Cynthia. She went to parochial school with Martha and they were best friends. I had never met her because she went away during the summer, but Martha was always talking about her. She had light-brown curls just like Shirley Temple's and lots of beautiful clothes because her father was rich. Her mother was dead and a maid took care of her and let her do anything she wanted to.

"That's very nice of you, Martha, to invite Allie for lunch," my mother said.

"We're having tuna fish sandwiches," Martha said. "They're Cynthia's favorite."

My mother looked at me. She knew I hated tuna fish because of the mayonnaise. I decided I would eat half a sandwich and then say I was full.

We went outside and tried to decide what we would do until lunchtime.

"I can't wait to see Cynthia," Martha said. "I've really missed her."

"Did you tell her about me?" I asked.

She shook her head. "I didn't talk to her all summer."

"You wrote her letters."

I thought it wasn't fair that Martha could have her pick of two best friends if she wanted to and I probably didn't even have one now that I didn't live in New Haven anymore.

"Let's go find some flowers in the field," Martha said. "Race you there!"

We ran out my driveway. Across the street Mimi was sitting on her stoop. A man was mowing the lawn. When we got to the field, Martha told me he was Mimi's father. She said he didn't live there anymore because he and Mimi's mother were getting a divorce. She said when he lived there they were always yelling at each other and that one time a policeman even came because they were disturbing the peace. Sonny Marco's father had called him.

Sonny Marco lived up at the corner. Even though I hadn't even met him yet, every time he saw me, he stuck out his tongue. Martha said he was a bully and to steer clear of him.

"And you know what else?" Martha said, almost in a whisper. "Promise you won't tell."

I crossed my heart.

"You've got to say it."

"Cross my heart and hope to die," I said.

"Mr. Minnick was arrested once. Nobody is supposed to know, but I heard my mother tell my father."

I felt a shiver. "Does Mimi know?"

"I guess she'd have to," Martha said. "It's her own father."

Now I really felt sorry for Mimi. Imagine having your father arrested.

"What did he do?" I asked.

"He's a bookie."

I knew what a bookie was. He was someone who took bets on horses. My father had a bookie named Mr. Schumaker who owned a candy store downtown.

"But why did they arrest him?" I asked.

"Because it's against the law. And he went to jail, too."

I never knew bookies were against the law. I wondered if my father knew. On the Saturdays when he couldn't go to the racetrack, he always called Mr. Schumaker up to make his bets after he had figured out which horses would probably win. You could also bet on horses to come in second, which was called place, or third, which was called show. Sometimes he let Danny and me help him choose. The horses had such great names: Seabiscuit, Man O'War, Bold Venture, War Admiral. And he had promised that he would take me to the races with him as soon as I was old enough.

He had given Danny a horse racing game for his birthday, even though our mother disapproved. She didn't like my father betting on horses. She said it was like throwing money down the drain.

By now Martha and I were at the gate. The field was covered with daisies. We started to pick them, watching out for the cow plops.

"You want to know something else?" she asked.

I nodded.

"I've never even told Cynthia about Mimi's father. You're the only one I've ever told."

So Martha and I had a secret from Cynthia. I liked that a lot.

chapter eleven

When we got back to Martha's house, Mimi's father was still mowing the lawn but Mimi wasn't there. I looked at him out of the corner of my eye. He didn't look like a person who had been in jail. He was wearing a shirt and a necktie and his hair was black and slicked back. He wasn't fat at all, not like Mimi and her mother. And he had a mustache.

"I think Mr. Minnick looks sort of like a movie star," I whispered to Martha.

"That's what my mother says. She think he looks like Clark Gable."

We both began to laugh and Mr. Minnick looked over at us.

"Hi, Mr. Minnick," Martha called.

"Hello, Martha." He walked across the street. "I haven't seen you for a long time. How's your family? How's Claire?"

"Everyone's fine, thank you," Martha said. Her face was

red. I knew she was wondering if Mr. Minnick had guessed we were talking about him.

"And who's your friend?"

"This is Allie. She just moved in next door."

Mr. Minnick smiled at me. His teeth were very white. "So you're Allie," he said. He really looked like a movie star when he smiled. "Mimi's told me all about you."

I wondered what she had said about me.

"She's only told me nice things," Mr. Minnick said as if he were reading my mind. He winked at me.

Now I felt my face getting red, too.

"We've got to go," Martha said. "Someone is coming over for lunch."

Mr. Minnick smiled at me again. "Nice meeting you, Allie," he said. "I'm glad you and Mimi are getting to be friends."

He walked back to his yard and started mowing the lawn again. Martha and I went into her house. Her mother gave us a vase for the flowers and we put them in the middle of the table. Then we went up to her room. Martha shut the door and looked at me. Without saying a word, we both burst out laughing again.

"He's so handsome," I said.

"I know," Martha said.

"But there's something a little scary about him, too," I said. "The way he could tell what I was thinking and everything."

"Shhh!" Martha whispered. "I hear someone." She opened her door and sure enough Claire was standing there.

"You were spying on us!"

Claire laughed. "I was not. I just came up to tell you Cynthia's here."

Martha raced downstairs and I followed slowly.

"Cynthia!"

"Martha!"

They threw their arms around each other and jumped up and down. Cynthia was just as pretty as Martha had said. She was wearing a blue playsuit and everything else matched, even her socks and the ribbon in her hair.

"I've got so much to tell you!" Cynthia said.

"Me, too!" Martha answered. "I really missed you."

"Me, too!" Cynthia said. "I kept wishing you could visit me. My father says I can invite you next summer."

Martha squealed and clapped her hands. "Goody!"

She finally remembered that I was there and introduced me.

"Hi," Cynthia said. "Are you going to St. John's?"

I shook my head.

"She isn't Catholic," Martha said.

"What are you?" Cynthia asked. "Are you a Protestant?"

"I'm Jewish."

A strange look passed over Cynthia's face. "Like Mimi Minnick?"

I didn't answer. We all went into the dining room. The table looked beautiful, with our daisies and a pink tablecloth and matching pink napkins.

"Allie and I picked the flowers this morning," Martha said. "Down in Mr. Sherwood's pasture."

"Ugh!" Cynthia said. "I hate going there with all those cow plops."

Mrs. Bryant came in with a plate full of sandwiches. They were cut in little triangles without any crusts.

"I made some chicken sandwiches, too," she said. "In case Allie doesn't like tuna fish." She smiled at me.

I helped myself to two sandwiches and some carrot sticks. Mrs. Bryant poured us each a glass of chocolate milk. It was my very favorite lunch.

Mrs. Bryant asked Cynthia if she had had a nice summer.

"It was all right," Cynthia said. "But I didn't like the house we rented this time. It wasn't as nice as the one we had last summer."

"Did you swim a lot?" Martha asked.

"Every day, just about, except when it rained. I got three new bathing suits."

Three new bathing suits. I only had one and it was from last year.

"What else did you do?" Martha asked.

"Oh, not much. I went out fishing with Nancy Donovan on her boat and I took tennis lessons with her at the club."

"Who's Nancy Donovan?"

"I wrote you all about her," Cynthia said. "She lived near us. We played together every day. She's really nice."

I looked at Martha. She was staring down at her plate. I put down my milk and took a deep breath.

"Martha and I played together every day, too," I said in a loud voice. Under the table I felt my knees shaking.

No one said anything. Mrs. Bryant brought in dessert, chocolate pudding with whipped cream. When I had finished, I folded my napkin and got up.

"I have to go," I said. I went out to the kitchen to thank Mrs. Bryant. She was washing the dishes.

"I'm sorry you have to leave so soon," she said.

I told her I had promised to play with Danny, which was a fib.

"What a nice big sister you are," she said. "We're so happy your family moved here." She handed me a dish covered with wax paper. "I made an awful lot of the chocolate pudding. Take some home for Danny."

On my way home I thought about Cynthia. What I thought was that even though she was pretty and rich I really didn't like her at all.

chapter twelve

"Home so early?" my mother asked, looking surprised. "I thought you were going to stay at Martha's all afternoon."

"Mrs. Bryant sent some chocolate pudding for Danny," I said, handing her the bowl.

"Isn't that kind of her," my mother said. "They're such a nice family."

Just then the doorbell rang. It was the mailman with a package.

"Are you Miss Alice Sherman?" he asked.

When I nodded, he said, "Then this parcel is for you. Sign here, please."

I took his pencil and wrote my name where he showed me. I had never signed for a package before. I had never gotten a package in the mail before, either.

I brought it into the kitchen. It was wrapped up in wrinkled brown paper and tied with string. It had lots of stamps on it. In the corner it said:

Mrs. Samuel Greenberg
54 Charlton St.
New Haven, Conn.

"Well, think of that!" my mother said. "Mrs. Greenberg has sent you a present, just like she promised."

I tried to guess what it would be. I hoped it was a dress. Last year she had made a really fancy pink party dress for Ruthie.

I tried to unknot the string but I couldn't, so I got the scissors and cut it. Then I opened the box. Inside was a folded-up thing made of polka-dotted material. The polka dots were purple. Even after I took it out and unfolded it, I wasn't sure what it was.

"Oh, how adorable!" my mother said. "They're bloomers!"

Bloomers? What were bloomers?

"Try them on," she said. "Let's see if they fit."

I took off my shorts and shirt and put them on. First you pulled up the bottom part and then you wiggled into the top. The legs and the sleeves both had elastic in them so that they puffed out. My mother fixed the collar and buttoned me up.

“They’re perfect!” she said. “Just like a playsuit. They’ll be perfect for your tap dancing class. Go to the mirror and see how nice you look.”

I went into the hall. Even before I saw what I looked like, I knew I hated them. The elastic was tight and made me feel itchy. When I saw myself in the hall mirror, I looked horrible. I stuck out my tongue.

“What’s the matter?” my mother asked. “Don’t you like them?”

“They’re awful! They’re not like a playsuit at all!”

I thought of Cynthia’s playsuit, all neat and trim. I knew she would never wear anything like this. Neither would Martha. They made me look like a baby.

“Don’t be silly,” my mother said. “Think of all the trouble Mrs. Greenberg went to.”

“I don’t care.” I said, pulling them off. “I won’t wear them.”

“Of course you will. There’s nothing wrong with them.” My mother folded them up and put them on the counter. “When Daddy gets home, we’ll show them to him. He’ll tell you how becoming they are.”

She sent me to go upstairs to get my writing paper so I could write Mrs. Greenberg a thank-you note. But after I had written “Dear Mrs. Greenberg, Thank you for the polka-dotted bloomers,” I couldn’t think of what else to say.

"Tell her that you like them," my mother said.

"But that's a lie," I said. That would make two lies in one day.

"Then tell her they fit perfectly."

"No, they don't," I said. "They're too tight."

"Allie!" my mother said in her warning voice. "Don't get me aggravated!"

When the letter was finished, I went up to my room. I really was disappointed about the bloomers. Ruthie should have told her mother how stupid they were. Maybe she hadn't seen them. But she had to have; their sewing machine was right in the kitchen.

And my mother was really being mean. Talk about lying. She could see how stupid they looked on me, so how could she say they didn't? When she showed them to my father, would he lie, too?

Danny came in.

"I saw what Mrs. Greenberg sent you," he said. "I thought she was going to make you a party dress. What are they anyway?"

When I didn't answer, he said, "They're funny-looking."

"I know," I said. "I hate them."

Danny wrinkled his nose. "I don't blame you. They're really awful."

Well, at least Danny understood.

chapter thirteen

The next morning I heard someone calling my name from the backyard. For a minute I thought it was Martha. But then I realized it was Mimi. I looked out the kitchen window and there she was, standing below the back porch and repeating my name again and again in a loud voice that could probably be heard all over the block.

I went outside. "You don't have to yell," I told her.

"I thought maybe you couldn't hear me," she said.

"The whole world could hear you. And you don't have to keep calling so long. You should wait to see whether somebody comes out."

"I'm sorry," she said, looking down her feet. "I was afraid you had forgotten we were going to play this morning."

"Of course I hadn't forgotten," I said, crossing my fingers.

"Do you want to play on your sidewalk or mine?"

"You mean hopscotch?" I asked. I thought of Martha seeing us or, even worse, Cynthia.

She nodded.

"I thought we could do something else for a change," I said. "Like paper dolls."

Her face lit up. "I love paper dolls! Should I go get mine?"

"We can play with mine today," I said. The minute I said it, I knew I'd made a mistake, but luckily she didn't notice and say we could play with hers tomorrow.

We went upstairs. Danny was standing in the hall, waiting for us.

Mimi smiled at him. "We're going to play paper dolls."

"Can I play, too?"

"Only girls play paper dolls," I told him. "Boys play with cars and trucks."

"You play cars and trucks with me sometimes," he said.

Mimi poked me. "Can't we let him play?" she whispered in my ear.

I shrugged. It probably wouldn't be much worse playing with Mimi and Danny together than playing with Mimi alone.

We all went into my room. I was glad I had already made my bed and put my dolls back in their places before breakfast. Mimi looked around, her eyes wide.

"It's just like a princess's room," she said. "Pink is my favorite color."

"Not mine," Danny said. "I think pink is yucky."

I gave him a look. "If you're not good, you can't play with us."

I went to my closet and got out my boxes of paper dolls. I kept each set in its own shoe box that I had decorated with pictures cut out from magazines. I had six boxes of dolls already cut out and another one with dolls I'd made myself. And I had two books that I hadn't cut out yet, a brand new Shirley Temple one and one with three babies that my Aunt Sadie had sent me last year for my birthday.

Mimi opened each box, examining the dolls and their clothes, trying to decide which ones to play with. Finally she chose the ones that were my favorites, too. They were the alphabet dolls and there were twenty-six of them, each named for a different letter except that there was no *X*. To make up for it, there were two *Q*s, twins, Queenie and Quentin. Danny liked the alphabet dolls, too, because there were lots of boys. I usually pretended that they were all brothers and sisters, but today we decided to take turns picking them and have three families. I had written their names on their backs. I lined them all up on the rug in alphabetical order.

We did one potato to see who went first and Mimi won.

She chose Irene, the only doll with red hair. Danny was second and he picked Quentin. I took Annabelle, the tallest. We went round and round until we each had eight and there were two left. I decided Mimi and I could have the extras because we were the oldest.

We started to play, building houses for them with Danny's blocks and visiting back and forth. Then Danny said we should take them all outside for a picnic. Mimi agreed.

I said I was afraid they would get dirty, but they both promised to be careful. Then I said it was probably too hot out, but they said it wasn't. I had just about run out of excuses why we shouldn't play outside when luckily my mother came to tell us it was lunchtime. Mimi said she'd better go home.

"Can't she have lunch with us?" Danny asked. "We're having so much fun!"

I looked at my mother. We hardly ever had anybody to lunch except for real company.

"Would you like to stay, Mimi?" my mother asked. "I'm afraid all we're having is tomato soup and peanut butter sandwiches."

Mimi said she loved tomato soup and peanut butter sandwiches. I could see a tiny smile flit across my mother's face and I knew what she was thinking. There probably weren't many foods Mimi didn't love. Then my mother told Mimi to telephone home and ask if she could stay. Mimi nodded but didn't move.

"Would you rather I called?" my mother asked.

Mimi nodded again.

We all went downstairs and my mother picked up the phone. "What's your number?" she asked.

"I'm not sure," Mimi said, biting her lip and looking embarrassed.

Even Danny knew our telephone number. My mother had taught it to him when we moved here.

My mother got the telephone book. "Here it is," she said. "498-2654. You really should learn your number," she told Mimi as she dialed. "It's very important." She waited a minute, listening. "Nobody answers," she said. "Was your mother going out?"

Mimi's face got red. "Sometimes she takes a nap," she mumbled.

Suddenly Danny spoke up. "Sometimes you take naps, too, don't you, Mommy?"

My mother smiled at him. "Sometimes," she said. "Whenever I get a chance."

My mother never took naps, so she was telling a fib. But somehow it didn't feel like one. She said that as long as Mimi's mother knew she was with us, she could stay for lunch and then they'd call later and explain.

As my mother set another place at the table and gave us each a bowl of soup and a sandwich, I remembered yesterday's lunch at Martha's. Even though ours wasn't as fancy, it made me feel happy to see that my mother was being just as nice to Mimi as Mrs. Bryant had been to me.

chapter fourteen

Mimi stayed a while after lunch. It had started raining so we couldn't go outside and have a picnic for the paper dolls. Instead we went back to Danny's room and built more houses. He really liked Mimi. After she went home and we were putting away the blocks, he kept talking about how much fun she was to play with.

I had to admit that we'd really had a good time together. When I thought about it, it reminded me of how I used to feel sometimes playing with Ruthie. And then I thought that I hardly ever felt that way with Martha. Maybe it was because Martha almost always decided what we were going to do. And some of my favorite things, like paper dolls and hopscotch, we hardly ever did because Claire said they were babyish. But I still liked Martha better than Mimi.

Later it stopped raining and my mother decided we would

walk downtown to buy my tap dancing shoes. I was really excited.

It was a pretty long walk and Danny got tired.

"Why can't we take the bus?" he whined, dragging his feet.

We both knew why we couldn't take the bus. It cost too much. Besides, our mother said walking was good for us. But we always asked anyway.

Finally we reached the shoe store. We all sat down and a salesman came over to measure my feet. When he smiled, his teeth were all yellow.

"Size five and a half narrow," he said. "Let's see if we have your size."

He came back with some boxes and sat down on his stool. He took a shoe out of a box and put my foot into it, using a silvery shoe horn. It was shiny black patent leather with a silky black ribbon that you tied in a bow.

"Stand up and see how that feels," he said.

I stood up.

"Now walk in it."

Even though it looked beautiful, it felt too tight.

"Never mind," he said. "I have it in a bigger size."

The next pair felt fine. My mother pressed the toe.

"Are you sure there's enough room?" she asked. "I don't want her to outgrow them too soon."

"You shouldn't get them too large," the salesman said. "Otherwise she won't be able to dance in them."

"Let her try on the next size just to be sure."

I felt embarrassed. I hated it when my mother did that. She was always buying us things that were too big so we could wear them for a long time.

The salesman came back without a box.

"Sorry," he said. "We're out of that size. But it would have been too big anyway."

"These are big enough," I said. "There's lots of room for my feet to grow."

"Well, all right," my mother said doubtfully. "But I would have felt better if you had been able to try on the larger pair."

We went to the cash register and she counted out some money. The salesman wrapped the shoe box in crispy white paper and tied it with some red string from a great big ball. The paper would be wonderful to draw on and the box could hold my Shirley Temple paper doll and her clothes.

We left the store and walked down the street to the ice cream parlor. We had only been there once before. Inside it was dark and cool. We sat down at the counter and Danny started spinning around on his stool until my mother made him stop.

"What'll it be?" the counterman asked us. He was dressed in white with a squashy white hat.

“Three cones,” my mother said.

“One or two scoops?”

“One will be fine.”

Danny made a face. “I want two.”

“All right, two,” my mother said.

I looked at my mother’s face. She hardly ever let us have two scoops.

“What flavor?”

“Can we have two different ones?” I asked.

The counterman nodded.

I read the flavors to Danny: chocolate, vanilla, strawberry, peach, maple walnut, and fudge ripple. He chose fudge ripple and chocolate and I picked vanilla and maple walnut. My mother got one scoop of chocolate.

The counterman began to scoop out the ice cream. The scoops were really big. After he handed us our cones and our mother paid him, she said that we should eat them inside so they wouldn’t melt.

“This is so yummy!” Danny said. He had chocolate ice cream on the tip of his nose and on his chin and he looked like a clown.

“It certainly hits the spot,” my mother said, “on such a hot day.”

After we had finished, we started walking home. On the

way a car tooted its horn and pulled up next to us. It was Daddy.

"Well, fancy meeting you here!" he said. "Hop in!"

We all got in and Danny told him about our ice cream cones. "Two scoops!" he said. "She let us have two scoops!"

"And I got my tap shoes," I told him.

"And Allie let me play with her and Mimi, the whole day," Danny said.

As we pulled up into our driveway, I saw Martha and Cynthia out on the sidewalk playing ball. Martha waved to me. I got out of the car and walked over to them.

"I called for you before," she said. "But you weren't home."

"We went to get my tap dancing shoes."

"Cynthia's staying for supper because it's Thursday."

I must have looked puzzled because Cynthia added, "Thursday is our maid's night off."

She said it as if I was stupid not to have known. Martha invited me to play with them and handed me the ball.

"We're up to F," she told me.

I started to bounce. "F my name is Frances, my husband's name is Frederick, I come from Florida, and I eat frankfurters."

"Good!" Martha said. "Do G."

I started bouncing again. "G my name is Gloria, my

husband's name is George, I come from Georgia, and I eat . . . gum."

"You lose," Cynthia said. "You can't eat gum." She reached out her hand for the ball. "My turn."

"You can so," I said. "If you swallow it, it's like eating it."

"It is not," she said. "It's not a food. It has to be a food. You're a cheater."

I threw the ball at her and it landed right in her stomach.

"Ow!' she yelled.

"You're mean!" I told her. "I don't care if I never play with you again!"

Cynthia glared at me. "Who would want to play with you, anyway?" she said. "You're a dirty Jew!"

At these words I felt my face begin to burn. It was as if I had been hit in the stomach, too. I looked at Martha, waiting for her to say something, but she didn't. I turned quickly and ran across her yard and up my driveway. The beautiful day, with paper dolls and new tap dancing shoes and two scoops of ice cream and Martha calling for me was all spoiled. I went in the back door. My father was sitting at the kitchen table, smoking and reading the newspaper.

"Well, Allie Oop," he said. "When are you going to put on your new shoes and dance for me?"

Without answering, I ran upstairs into my room, slamming the door behind me.

chapter fifteen

I threw myself on my bed and buried my face in my pillow. My pink pillow. All of a sudden I hated it and everything else that was pink, my bed and my rug and my room, everything. But most of all I hated Strawberry Hill. Why had we ever moved here? Why couldn't we have stayed in New Haven and gone on living with the Greenbergs? Why did I have to leave Ruthie and my other friends and come to a place with people like Cynthia? I hated her. I hadn't done anything to her and suddenly out of the blue she started calling me names. I knew I threw the ball hard but she could have caught it and anyway it was just a little rubber one. And anyway I only did it because she said I was a cheater. But that wasn't as bad as the other thing she called me. No one had ever called me that before.

My mother yelled that supper was ready, but I didn't move. After a few minutes I heard her opening my door.

"Didn't you hear me? It's time for supper."

"I'm not hungry."

"What do you mean, you're not hungry? What's the matter?"

"Nothing."

"Something's the matter. What is it?"

"I had a fight with Cynthia," I mumbled into my pillow.

"What kind of fight?"

I turned my head and looked up at her. I started to cry. "She called me a dirty Jew."

My mother's eyes narrowed. "What?"

I told her about the fight and how Cynthia started it by saying I was a cheater and how she missed the ball and it hit her in the stomach. But I could tell that she wasn't really listening to what I was saying. The only thing she cared about was what Cynthia had called me.

She lifted me up and led me over to my mirror. "Look at yourself," she said, kneeling down beside me. "You're a beautiful little girl. I don't want you ever to forget that."

She had never said anything like that to me before. For a moment we both stared at our faces pressed close together, hers pale and unsmiling, mine red with swollen eyes. Then we stood up and went downstairs, holding hands. In the kitchen Danny and my father were already eating.

"What's going on?" my father asked.

"We'll be right back," my mother said. Without another word she hurried out the door, pulling me along beside her. When we got to the Bryants, she knocked loudly at their back door. Mrs. Bryant opened it.

"Is something the matter?" she asked, looking surprised.

"There certainly is," my mother said. "Is Cynthia here?"

"Why, yes," Mrs. Bryant said. "She and Martha are playing upstairs."

"I'd like to see her right now," said my mother.

"Is anything wrong?"

"Cynthia called Allie a nasty name and I'd like to speak to her about it."

We stood there in the Bryants' kitchen, not saying anything. I was scared, wondering what was going to happen.

Mrs. Bryant came back with Cynthia, who was scowling. Martha trailed after them. But even though I looked straight at her, she wouldn't look back at me.

My mother went over to Cynthia. "I hear you called my daughter a dirty Jew."

Cynthia glared at me. "She threw a ball at me and hit me in the stomach," she said. "And she cheated."

"I did not!" I said.

"You did so!"

My mother ignored all this and repeated her question. "Did you or didn't you call her a dirty Jew?"

"I don't remember," Cynthia said sullenly, looking away.

My mother pushed me over in front of Cynthia.

"Look at her!" she demanded.

When Cynthia didn't look up, my mother repeated in a louder voice, "I said to look at her!"

Slowly Cynthia raised her eyes.

"Is she dirty?" my mother asked. "Is my daughter dirty?"

"Uh-uh," Cynthia mumbled.

"Then why did you say she was?"

"I don't know."

"If you were my child, I would wash out your mouth with soap. That's the place that's dirty."

Cynthia's face grew red. But my mother hadn't finished.

"I want you to understand something," she said. "You can be dirty on the outside or you can be dirty on the inside. Outside dirt can be washed off. But when you call people names that insult their religion, you're dirty on the inside. And that's not washed away so easily."

Her voice broke and she stopped, her face flushed. Mrs. Bryant patted her shoulder and turned to Cynthia.

"I'm sure you'd like to apologize," she said.

Cynthia pinched her lips together.

"Just tell Allie and her mother that you're sorry for what you said. You see how upset they are."

Cynthia mumbled something.

"Now why don't you and Allie shake hands."

Reluctantly we stuck our hands out, then immediately pulled them away. I looked over at Martha again but she still refused to meet my eye.

"Good," Mrs. Bryant said, looking relieved. "Now you can put all this behind you and be friends again."

"Can I go home now?" Cynthia asked.

"Your father's picking you up in an hour," Mrs. Bryant said.

"But I want to go home right now."

"I'll call and see if he can come sooner," Mrs. Bryant said. "Why don't you and Martha go upstairs until he gets here."

After Cynthia and Martha left, Mrs. Bryant let out a deep sigh. "I can't tell you how sorry I am about all this, Mrs. Sherman," she said. "She probably just repeated something she heard."

"I'm sure she did," my mother replied. "I had hoped this sort of thing wouldn't happen around here. But I was wrong."

Mrs. Bryant frowned. "You mustn't think . . . I mean, we're so glad you and your family are living next door. I just want you to know that."

"Thank you," my mother said.

"She's just a child," Mrs. Bryant continued. "And very

spoiled. But Allie's told you about her family situation, I imagine. Of course that doesn't excuse her behavior."

"No, it doesn't," my mother answered.

"I think she's learned a lesson."

"I hope so," my mother replied.

Walking back home, holding my mother's hand, I was miserable. Even though she had defended me, I wished the whole thing had never happened. I was ashamed that she had yelled and lost her temper in front of Mrs. Bryant, who was always so quiet and polite. And I was embarrassed about how she had talked to Cynthia. I knew that she had spoiled everything. Because no matter what Mrs. Bryant said, it was silly to think that Cynthia had learned a lesson and that we could be friends again. The only lesson she had learned was not to call me bad names to my face.

When we got home, Danny and my father were eating dessert.

"Now, what was that all about?" my father asked.

My mother glanced at Danny, shook her head, and whispered something in my father's ear.

"What did you tell Daddy?" Danny asked.

"Nothing," my mother said. She turned to my father. "I knew that would happen in this kind of neighborhood. It was only a matter of time."

"Oh, come on," my father said. "I was called worse when I was a kid."

"What do you mean?" my mother asked angrily. "How can you say that?"

"Calm down. It's only a kids' squabble. I think you overreacted."

"Overreacted? What should I have done?"

"Probably nothing," my father said. "Come here, Allie Oop," he said to me, patting his lap. "Always remember sticks and stones."

I climbed onto his lap and finished, "Can break my bones, but names can never hurt me."

My mother brought over a big plate of reheated spaghetti and meatballs and, even though I had thought I wasn't hungry, I finished the whole thing.

chapter sixteen

That night Danny and I were both allowed to stay up until eight o'clock. My father played us two games of Parcheesi and my mother read us "Puss in Boots," Danny's favorite fairy tale, and "Clever Gretel," which was mine. But when I went to bed, I couldn't fall asleep.

The light was still on in Martha's bedroom, which was right across from mine. Sometimes we sat at our windows and called over to each other, and we had been planning to run a string between them so that we could send each other secret messages. But we probably wouldn't ever do that now. We probably wouldn't even play together anymore.

Martha's light went out. By now it was almost dark. The green leaves of the maple tree right outside my window had turned black. Through their cracks I could see the moon. Usually I liked to pick out faces among the leaves from the moon sparkles, mouths with shiny smiles and bright eyes twinkling at me. But tonight the faces looked scary, like black masks with burning holes for eyes.

I could hear a kind of rumbling from downstairs and I knew that my mother and father were arguing. Even though I couldn't hear what they were saying, I knew it was about what had happened.

I got out of bed and tiptoed to the top of the stairs.

". . . let her fight her own battles." That was my father.

"If it were up to you, you'd ignore everything."

"Well, that's a lot better than making a mountain out of a molehill!"

"Since when is anti-Semitism a molehill?"

"They were kids, having a squabble. Without you interfering, it would have blown over. Now it's a big deal."

"So what would you have done?"

"Talked to her about it. Not run off half-cocked next door."

"Half-cocked?" My mother was screaming. "With all that's going on in the world?"

"Oh, for Christ's sake! This is some stupid kid repeating some stupid thing she heard on the playground!" Now my father was yelling, too.

Suddenly I heard footsteps and I ran back to bed. I had just pulled the covers up over my head when my door opened.

"Allie?" It was my father.

I pretended to be asleep.

"You were listening, weren't you?" He pulled my blanket away and ruffled my hair. "You can't fool me, little spy."

"What's anti-Semitism?" I asked.

"It's prejudice against Jewish people. Other people not liking Jews."

"Why?"

"It's a long story. But anti-Semitism is stupid. And people who are anti-Semites are stupid people."

"Like Cynthia?"

"Sometimes kids just repeat things they hear without knowing what they mean."

His voice trailed off. "I probably was too hard on your mother."

"I don't like you to fight."

"I know. But sometimes we do. It doesn't mean we don't love each other." He smiled at me. "Do you want to know something interesting?"

"Uh huh."

"Jesus was a Jew. The next time you see Cynthia, you tell her that. You tell her to put that in her pipe and smoke it."

He kissed me goodnight. And the next thing I knew, it was morning.

chapter seventeen

The next day I stayed inside all morning, playing with my paper dolls on the living room rug. Usually it would have been fun, but today it wasn't. I kept hoping Martha would call for me. Every few minutes I would peek out from behind the curtains to see if she was outside, but she never was. I saw Claire going off somewhere on her bicycle and Mrs. Bryant sweeping their front stoop, but I never saw Martha.

School was going to start in two weeks. Earlier in the summer, when it seemed far away, I was excited about it. But now that it was so close, I felt sort of scared. We had already gone downtown to buy a new dress for me to wear the first day. It was pink and all flouncy and fancy, like the one I had hoped Mrs. Greenberg would make me, but she had made those horrible bloomers instead. And my father had bought me a new pencil box with a ruler and five red pencils and a big pink eraser. But I was worried. Mimi would probably want to walk with me and what if that made everybody think she was my best friend? Then maybe nobody else would want to be friends with me.

I went to the window again and there she was, as if thinking about her had made her appear. She was crossing the street and walking up our driveway. Danny ran into the living room.

"Mimi's here!" he said. "She's calling for you."

"I don't feel good," I said. "Tell her I can't come out."

"But you do feel good," Danny said. "You've been playing all morning."

"No, I don't. I've got a stomachache. You can play by yourself when you've got one but not with other people."

Danny made a face. "You're fibbing. You just don't want to play with Mimi."

"So what if I don't?" I said.

"But Mimi's fun. Funner than Martha."

"She is not!" I said.

A few minutes later I saw Mimi through the window, going home again. Her shoulders were all hunched over. Even from the back, I could tell she was disappointed. I went over to the front door, opened it, and called her. She turned around in the middle of the street.

"Do you want to play?" I called.

Mimi ran over. "Danny said you had a stomachache."

"I did but it's better," I said, not looking at Danny. "What do you want to do?"

"I know what," Danny said. "Let's go down to the field and see the cows." He could only do that when someone older went with him.

"That's a good idea, Danny!" Mimi said enthusiastically. "I wish I had a little brother like you."

Danny beamed. What a funny thing to say, I thought. But the funniest thing of all was that Mimi really meant it.

When we got to the field, we saw Mr. Sherwood going into the barn. He waved to us and invited us to come inside.

"I'm just about to milk the cows," he said. "Would you like to help?"

We all said yes. First we washed our hands. Then we watched as Mr. Sherwood sat down on a low stool next to Sally and washed off her udder with water and a rag. Next he put a tin bucket under her and began to squeeze. Pretty soon milk started dripping into the pail.

Mr. Sherwood stood up. "Who wants to go first?"

I raised my hand and Mr. Sherwood laughed.

"Well, give it a try," he said.

I sat down on the stool and took hold of Sally's udder. It was soft, with little hairs sticking out of it, and I could feel the milk swooshing around inside.

"Now just squeeze and pull down," Mr. Sherwood said.

I did but nothing happened.

"Squeeze a little harder. You won't hurt her. She likes to be milked."

Finally a few drops came out.

"Now you've got the hang of it," Mr. Sherwood said. "Who's next?"

Mimi sat down and managed to get a few more drops. Then it was Danny's turn. Mr. Sherwood bent over him and placed his hands on the udder. A big gush of milk splashed down into the pail.

"Well, look at that!" Mr. Sherwood said. "I think we've got a farmer here!"

Danny grinned. Mr. Sherwood winked at us.

"How would you like a taste?" he asked. He took a ladle and dipped some milk out of the bucket. Each of us took a swallow. It was warm and creamy and sweet.

"It doesn't even taste like milk," Danny said.

"Oh, yes, it does," said Mr. Sherwood. "That's what real milk tastes like, straight from the cow. It's the milk you get in bottles that doesn't taste like milk. They boil all the flavor out of it."

We watched as Mr. Sherwood finished milking Sally and began to milk Bessie. Then we thanked him and started to walk home. Danny couldn't stop talking about what Mr. Sherwood had said.

"I'm a farmer!" he bragged. "Mr. Sherwood said so!"

"He was only fooling," I said. "How can someone five years old be a farmer?"

"He said so! He said I'm the best milker!"

Mimi smiled at me. "Yes, you are, Danny," she said. "You milked Sally better than we did."

"See!" Danny said. "Mimi knows!"

I was getting a little tired of Danny liking Mimi so much. And I knew that if she had to live with him all the time, she wouldn't think he was so cute either.

When we got home, we tried to decide what to do next. It had gotten really hot out so we decided to play inside.

We were just going in when Martha came out her front door and walked over.

"Hi, Allie!"

I was really surprised. Her voice sounded friendly, just as if nothing had happened.

"Hi."

"What are you all doing?"

"We're going to play games," Danny answered before I could say anything.

"Could I play, too?" Martha asked.

"Sure," I said.

We all went up to my room.

"Well, what do you want to play?" I asked.

"Let's play the horse racing game," Danny said.

There were five horses with jockeys and each player would pick a horse to bet on. Then someone cranked the handle and the horses would run around the track and you never knew which one would win. It was really exciting.

But just as I was about to say okay, I saw Mimi's face. The old crybaby face. And all of a sudden I remembered about her father.

"I'd rather play cards," I said. "We can play the horse racing game another time."

Danny looked disappointed.

"We'll play Crazy Eights," I announced. It was his favorite card game and he was really good at it.

Mimi looked relieved. We all sat down on my pink rug. And even though Danny was good, Mimi was better. She won almost every game.

"You've got a good memory," Martha said to her. I could see that she was impressed.

"It's because I've played a lot with my father," Mimi said. "He loves cards. Especially pinochle."

That was our father's favorite game, too. He played it with his friends every Tuesday night. It was funny to think of him and Mr. Minnick enjoying the same things, like pinochle and betting on horses, when otherwise they were so different.

chapter eighteen

We played games all afternoon. Then, when Martha and Mimi were ready to go home, Martha said she had to go to the bathroom.

By the time she came back, Mimi had left and Danny had gone downstairs. For a minute Martha didn't say anything. She just stood there staring at me. Then all of a sudden she started crying. I was really surprised. I had never seen her cry before. I didn't think she ever had anything to cry about. But then, without knowing exactly why, I began to cry, too.

"I'm sorry about yesterday," she said.

"It wasn't your fault."

"Cynthia was mean."

I took a deep breath. "You don't think that, do you?"

"Think what?"

"You know . . . what Cynthia called me."

Martha looked shocked. "Of course not! You're my friend."

"What about Cynthia?" I asked.

"She's not allowed to come over anymore."

"Did your mother say that?"

Martha shook her head. "Her father. He called up last night and yelled at my mother. He was really mad." She wiped her eyes. "But I don't care. Besides, I like you better anyway."

I couldn't believe her, even though I wanted to. I thought that she was just sad because Cynthia couldn't come over. And in a way I didn't blame her. After all, Cynthia hadn't been mean to her. And they had been best friends for a long time. But maybe, after what Cynthia had said, Martha really didn't like her so much anymore.

All of a sudden I felt really happy, so happy that I started to laugh. Martha stared at me for a minute, and then she started laughing, too. We threw our arms around each other and began twirling around the room until we were so dizzy we fell down on my bed.

My mother came in to see what was going on.

"There was so much noise I thought the ceiling would cave in," she said. "What in the world were you girls doing?"

We burst out giggling.

After Martha went home, my mother sat down on my bed. "Come here," she said, patting the place beside her. I sat down and she put her arm around me.

"Mrs. Bryant called a little while ago," she said. Noticing my worried look, she added, smiling, "Don't worry. I didn't lose my temper again."

I felt relieved. "What did she want?"

"She told me that Cynthia's father called her last night to find out what had happened."

"He was mad, wasn't he?"

My mother looked surprised that I knew. "Why, yes, he was. But the awful thing was that he wasn't angry at Cynthia, he was angry at poor Mrs. Bryant. He told her she had no right to scold his daughter or allow anyone else to or to make her apologize for anything. And when Mrs. Bryant asked him if he knew what Cynthia had said, he said he didn't give . . ." She stopped herself, then continued, ". . . he said it didn't matter. What a horrible man!"

"I was wrong about Mrs. Bryant," she went on, almost as if she was talking to herself. "Sometimes you misjudge people. . . ."

"What?" I asked when she stopped.

"I guess I thought that she was making excuses for Cynthia and that it meant she was anti-Semitic herself. I was absolutely wrong."

She stood up. "I'll go start supper. Meatloaf and mashed potatoes."

My favorites. Of course we'd have canned peas, too, which I hated, but I could hide them in the potatoes and swallow them without chewing.

I curled up on my bed and looked out my window at the maple tree. Some of its leaves were beginning to turn yellow. Pretty soon it would be fall and it would be time to go back to school. To a new school.

chapter *nineteen*

The next morning, while I was eating breakfast, someone knocked at the back door. I opened it and saw a strange man with a dirty face and raggedy clothes standing there. He asked me if my mother was home. I knew I wasn't supposed to talk to strangers, but that was on the street. This was on my back porch.

When I told my mother who was there, she didn't seem surprised. She went out on the porch to talk to him. Then she came back into the kitchen and made two fat American cheese and lettuce and tomato sandwiches with lots of mayonnaise. She handed me a tall glass of milk and we brought everything outside.

The man was sitting on the steps, his eyes closed. When he heard us, he stood up and took off his cap and smiled. His teeth were all brown.

"Thank you, ma'am," he said in a soft voice. He looked over at the table uncertainly.

"Please sit down and enjoy your meal," my mother said.

I had never seen anyone eat so fast in my life. He gobbled down both sandwiches in a few bites, stuffing them into his mouth and hardly chewing. Then he gulped down the milk. After he had finished, he asked my mother if she minded if he smoked. When she said he could, he took a half-cigarette out of his pocket and lit it.

He told us he was from Maine. He had worked in a factory, but it had closed two years ago. After that he left Maine, looking for work.

"But there ain't no work," he said. He took a last puff of his cigarette, snuffed it out on the floor carefully, then put it back into his pocket. My mother brought the empty plate and glass back to the kitchen and returned with two packages of my father's Lucky Strike cigarettes. When she handed them to him, his eyes filled with tears.

"Thank you, ma'am," he said again. "That's really kind of you."

He walked slowly down the porch stairs, his back all slumped over. When he reached the driveway, he turned and waved at us.

"Good luck!" my mother called after him.

"Who was that?" I asked.

"A hobo," my mother said.

"What's a hobo?"

"It's a person who doesn't have a job because of the Depression so he travels around on the railroad looking for work."

I remembered in New Haven when my father didn't have a job.

"Would Daddy have been a hobo if he couldn't find work?"

"That's why we had to move to Stamford, because he couldn't find work in New Haven," she said, not answering my question.

"I miss New Haven," I said. Most of all, I thought, I missed the Greenbergs, but I didn't say that out loud.

"I do, too," my mother said. "I didn't think I would, but I do sometimes."

"Will the Depression ever be over?"

"I certainly hope so."

A little while later Martha came over to call for me. We went out to the porch and started swinging on the glider. I told her about the hobo and she said one had come to her house, too, a few months ago.

"It must be awful to be poor," I said.

Martha nodded. For a while we swung back and forth without talking.

"It's funny," Martha said to me after a while. "Mimi and I have lived across the street from each other since we were little and we never were friends until you moved here."

"Maybe it was because of Cynthia," I said. I felt uncomfortable saying her name. We never talked about her.

Martha shook her head. "I didn't ever like Mimi, even before I met Cynthia. Remember I told you that she smelled?"

I nodded.

"I only said that because all the other kids did. But she was always such a crybaby. And then her father went away and her mother is so weird and everything."

"Well, now you're friends with her," I said. "We both are."

"But not best friends," Martha said.

"Of course not! I'd never be best friends with her."

We looked at each other.

"Do you want to be best friends with me?" Martha asked.

I nodded. "Do you?"

We shook on it.

"We don't have to tell anybody," Martha said. "When Cynthia and I . . ." she stopped, looking embarrassed. "I mean, when you decide to be best friends with somebody, you should make up a secret password or something like that."

"When Ruthie and I were best friends, we gave each other secret names," I said.

"That's a great idea! What were they?"

I hesitated. Ruthie and I had sworn never to tell anybody. But since we weren't best friends anymore, maybe it was all right to tell Martha. After all, she was my new best friend, and best friends told each other everything.

"She was Mrs. Frome and I was Mrs. Cobble."

Martha giggled. "That's funny! Why did you pick those?"

"We just liked them. They were our names when we played house."

"Well, what should we be?"

We thought for a while. Then Martha had an idea. She said we could spell our names backward. She would be Ahtram Neleh Tnayrb and I would be Ecila Haras Namrehs. But when we started calling each other by these names, we burst out laughing, they sounded so goofy. And besides they were way too long. So we decided to use just our middle names. Martha was Neleh and I was Haras.

"Now remember," Martha said. "It's a secret. We can never ever tell anybody."

We crossed our hearts and hoped to die.

chapter twenty

The night before school started, I couldn't fall asleep for a long time. I kept worrying about what was going to happen, whether some kids would be mean to me, whether I would make any friends. I had seen Center School from the outside, but I had never been inside it. It was three stories high and made out of dark red brick, just like my old school. But it had a high fence all around it and it was in a different kind of neighborhood. Instead of houses like in New Haven, there were stores and gas stations and some old boarded-up buildings. It looked a little scary.

The next morning I woke up really early. My mother came into my room, still in her nightgown. She asked me how I was feeling. I said I wasn't exactly sure.

"I understand," she said. "You're feeling apprehensive. It's only natural to feel a little apprehensive on the first day at a new school."

I had never heard that word before, but it sounded just right. I repeated it to myself as I started to get dressed: ap-pre-hen-sive. I got out my writing folder and added it to the list on my word animals page: appreHENsive. I had already collected some others: COWard; DOGged; sCATter; BULLet; sPIGot; scalLION.

We had laid out all my clothes the night before. But when I put on my new dress, I decided I didn't really like it after all. It felt stiff and crackly. I opened my closet door and examined all my other dresses. Finally I decided on the light blue one with the white collar. It was pretty old and the hem had been let down, but it was still one of my favorites. I liked it because it was soft, and anyway you could hardly see where the old hemline had been.

When I went down to breakfast, my mother looked surprised. "Why are you wearing that?" she asked.

I told her my new dress was too fancy.

"Don't be silly," she said. "You picked it out yourself. Go back upstairs and put it on."

"Let her wear what she wants," my father said impatiently. "It's time to go."

He was going to drive me to school the first day. After lunch my mother was going to take Danny to his first day of afternoon kindergarten. After that I would have to walk to school with Mimi in the morning and with Mimi and Danny in the afternoon coming home.

My mother frowned. I could tell she was annoyed. But she just told me to hurry up and eat my cereal. I said I wasn't hungry because I was apprehensive.

She smiled. "Well, even so, you can't go to school on an empty stomach," she said. "At least drink some milk."

I took a few swallows, then put down my glass and kissed my mother good-bye. My father and I went out to the car.

"Can I go to your office with you?" I asked him.

He burst out laughing. "Come on, now," he said. "It's going to be just fine. Do you want me to come inside with you and help you find your room?"

I nodded.

"You worry too much about things," he said. "There's an expression for that — don't borrow trouble. Right now you're borrowing trouble. For all you know, this might turn out to be the most wonderful day of your life."

"Oh, Daddy, that's stupid!"

"Are you calling your one and only father stupid? The father who puts bread in your mouth and oatmeal on the table in a blue Shirley Temple bowl?"

Despite myself, I giggled. But at the same time I felt almost like crying. When we got to school, my father parked the car and we walked to the front door. All the other kids were standing in line, the boys on one side and the girls on the other. As we passed them, some of them stared at me or whispered to each other. Nobody smiled.

We went inside. My father looked around for a minute, then took my hand and led me to a door with a frosted glass window that said "Principal's Office." He knocked.

"Come in!" said a cheerful voice.

He opened the door and went in. There at a desk facing us was an old lady with white hair in braids around her head and rosy cheeks. And she was smiling as if she was really happy to see us.

"You must be Alice Sherman," she said. "I'm Mrs. Russell. You're the only new girl we have this year at Center. Three new boys but only one new girl, which makes you very special."

She opened a folder on her desk and shuffled through the pages. "Oh, yes, Alice. You're going to be in Miss Kerns's class. Why don't you come with me and I'll introduce you before the other children come in."

My father bent over to kiss me good-bye. As he did, he whispered in my ear, "What did I tell you? Don't borrow trouble."

I followed Mrs. Russell down the hall to Miss Kerns's room and found her writing something on the blackboard. When she heard us, she turned around.

Miss Kerns was tall and thin and her cheeks were as pink as Mrs. Russell's but you could tell hers were from rouge.

"Excuse me, Mrs. Russell," she said. "I was just finishing something."

Before I could read what she had written, she covered it up with a big piece of cardboard.

"Now then," she said, looking at me closely. "Who is this?"

Mrs. Russell introduced us. Miss Kerns didn't even smile. She just said she was pleased to meet me and pointed to where my desk was. Then she began talking to Mrs. Russell as if I wasn't even there.

I went to my desk and sat down. All my worries about school came back again. Even though Miss Kerns had said she was pleased to meet me, she certainly didn't act like it. And besides, she was really funny looking. With her straight skinny back and her tight bun of black hair, she reminded me a little of Popeye's girlfriend Olive Oyl.

After Mrs. Russell left, Miss Kerns sat down at her desk, went through some papers, and then looked up.

"I see you're from New Haven," she said. "What school did you go to there?"

I told her it was The Ben Franklin School.

"What a coincidence!" she said. "I did my teacher training at The Ben Franklin School. Did you know Mrs. Fine?"

"She was my first-grade teacher!" I said excitedly. "She

was really nice!" The minute I said it, I felt embarrassed, because it sounded as if I meant that Miss Kerns wasn't. Which I guess I did. But luckily she didn't seem to notice.

Instead she smiled for the very first time. "Mrs. Fine was my mentor at the Ben Franklin School. If you ever go back there, you must give her my regards."

I nodded, even though I didn't know what a mentor was or exactly how to give regards.

Suddenly we heard a commotion outside the door. Miss Kerns walked over and opened it. There were a bunch of kids out in the hall, talking and laughing with each other.

"Good morning," she said to them, a stern look on her face. It was hard to believe she had ever smiled. "I am Miss Kerns. Please come in."

chapter twenty-one

Suddenly everyone stopped talking at once. It was as if Miss Kerns had waved a magic wand.

"Please wait at the front of the room while I take attendance and tell you where your desks are."

They all filed in. They were all so quiet you could hear a pin drop. Some of them stared at me as I sat all alone in the middle of the fifth row.

Miss Kerns took a sheet of paper from her desk and began to read.

"Janet Anderson."

A short girl with stringy brown hair raised her hand. Miss Kerns pointed to the first seat in the first row, over by the windows.

"Dante Borelli."

"Dan. My name is Dan," a boy said. He had a crew cut of reddish-brown hair and freckles, and his ears stuck out.

Without answering, Miss Kerns motioned him over to the desk next to Janet's.

"Antoinette Buzzeo. Leonard Dunn. Peter Green."

One after another, they took their seats.

"Michael Johnson. Bruce Lojinsky. Alice Moran."

Another Alice! I had never had another Alice in my class before. While Miss Kerns's voice droned on, I studied the back of Alice Moran's head. She was sitting right in front of me, two rows away. She must have felt me looking at her because she turned around.

But before I could even smile at her, I heard Miss Kerns say, "Alice Sherman."

What was I supposed to do? I was at my desk already. Everyone was looking at me and I could feel my face getting red.

"Alice Sherman has just moved to Stamford," Miss Kerns said. "This is her first day at Center School. I want everyone to make her feel welcome. Especially Alice Moran, since they share the same first name. Allie, will you show Alice around the school at recess?"

For a minute I was confused. How could I show someone around the school when I had never been here before? And why would I have to show someone around who went here already? Then all of a sudden I realized what had happened.

I wasn't Allie anymore, Alice Moran was. She had first dibs on the name and from now on I would have to be Alice. But how could I be? I was Allie. Only people who didn't know me called me Alice.

By now Miss Kerns had finished the attendance and everybody had sat down. She clapped her hands.

"Now then," she said. "The next order of business is to get everybody's names straight. Dante has told us he prefers to be called Dan."

"I am Dan," Dante said loudly. "Everyone calls me Dan."

"Thank you, Dan," Miss Kerns said. She looked around the room. "Anyone else?"

I felt my arm lifting itself up.

"Yes, Alice?"

"I . . . my . . ." I stopped, confused. My voice was trembling.

"Yes?" Miss Kerns sounded impatient.

"My name . . . I'm called . . ." Alice Moran had turned around and was looking at me, a funny little smile on her face. Had she guessed?

"Allie!" I finally blurted out. "Everyone calls me Allie."

Miss Kerns nodded. "That is a problem," she said. "I wonder what we can do about it. You're sure you don't want to be called Alice?"

I shook my head vehemently.

Alice Moran raised her hand. "I can be Allie M and she can be Allie S if she wants to," she said in a soft voice.

"That's a very generous offer," Miss Kerns said. She looked at me. "What do you say, Alice?"

"It's fine," I said. Now I was smiling, too.

"Then Allie S you are," Miss Kerns said. "And Allie M *you* are," she said to Allie Moran.

She walked over to the blackboard.

"Now before we get down to work, I have a few classroom rules I want to impress upon you. I've written them on the blackboard and I'll leave them there until Friday so you can become familiar with them. But by the time I erase them, I'll expect you all to know them by heart. And as long as you follow them, we'll all get along very well together. Do you understand?"

In a chorus we answered, "Yes, Miss Kerns."

"Very well, then," she said. She removed the cardboard from the blackboard.

chapter twenty-two

In big letters was written:

MISS KERNS'S RULES OF CONDUCT
FOR HER FOURTH-GRADE STUDENTS

"Now then," Miss Kerns said. "I would like you to recite these rules aloud."

We all started to read at different speeds, some people mumbling, others in loud sing-songy voices. You couldn't understand a word. Miss Kerns clapped her hands.

"Stop!" she ordered. "It is important that you listen to each other and speak in unison. And you must use your best voices, not too soft and not too loud. Now when I clap, please start again."

This time it was better:

MISS KERNS'S RULES OF CONDUCT
FOR HER FOURTH-GRADE STUDENTS

1. No talking without permission.
2. No whispering or giggling in class.
3. No touching other people except during games.
4. No leaving your desk without permission.
5. No note passing.
6. Inkwells are only to be used for penmanship lessons. Otherwise they must be kept covered.

Everybody was so intent on reading properly that it wasn't until we had reached Rule 6 that someone started to laugh. It was Allie M. When we got to Rule 7, we saw what she was laughing at:

7. No lambs at school except by permission of the teacher.

The whole class burst out laughing. Miss Kerns looked as if she wanted to laugh, too, but she didn't let herself. She just pressed her lips together and told us to repeat Rule 2 in our best voices. Then she dismissed us for recess.

We divided ourselves into two lines, boys and girls, and filed out into the corridor. The boys went in one direction and the girls in another. Miss Kerns took Allie M and me aside and told Allie M to show me where the bathrooms were and the gym and the assembly hall. Then we were to join the rest of the class on the playground.

"I wonder if she's always like that," I said to Allie M after Miss Kerns had left us.

"Everyone says she's a little weird. My cousin had her two years ago and he was always telling funny stories about what happened in her room. He told me about the rules. Every year she makes up a new Number Seven."

"So that's why you laughed before we read it?"

"Uh-huh. But she's a really good teacher. My cousin was a terrible reader when he came into her class and by the end of the year he could read almost anything. He says her bark is worse than her bite."

I told Allie M about my father telling me not to borrow trouble. She had never heard that one before.

"It's like what I thought before I got here," I explained. "I was afraid I wasn't going to make any friends."

"And now you have," she said, smiling at me. "Me."

"That was really nice of you to let me be Allie, too," I said.

"I knew how you felt," she said. "I hate it when people call me Alice."

We headed out to the playground. As we walked outside, I thought of everything that had happened so far that morning. First of all, I had learned not to borrow trouble. Second, I now knew Miss Kerns's bark was worse than her bite. And best of all, I had made a brand-new friend who had the same name I did.

And recess wasn't even over.

chapter twenty-three

Out on the playground we went over to the girls' side together. At my old school the girls' side was on the left, but here it was on the right. We swung on the swings for a while and then we played hopscotch. I told her about how I had taught Mimi to play better. Allie M said that was great.

"Last year Mimi hardly ever played during recess. She always said she was too tired or had just been sick or something. But I think it was really because no one wanted her on their team."

Poor Mimi. It was awful being picked last for teams. I wondered if that would happen to me now that I was at a new school.

Allie M asked me why we had moved to Stamford. I told her about my father and his job.

"My father lost his job, too," she said. "Only he couldn't find another one. So he moved away."

"You're like Mimi," I said. "Her father doesn't live with her, either. But her parents are getting divorced."

"Mine aren't," Allie M said. "My father just went away one day and never came back."

"Where did he go?"

"We don't know. Every once in a while he sends us a post-card, but it's always from a different place. And sometimes he sends us some money."

So now I knew about three people who had lost their jobs because of the Depression: my father, the hobo, and Allie M's father. Only my father was lucky and had gotten another one. I wondered if Allie M's father had become a hobo, too, but I didn't want to ask. I could see it made her sad to talk about him.

Over on the boys' side I saw Dan playing marbles. Just as I looked at him, he lifted up his head and turned to look at me. Then he waved.

Allie M giggled. "Dan likes you."

"He does not!"

"Oh, yes, he does. I can tell."

Just then the bell rang. We hurried over to the side door to get in line. Allie M poked me.

"You've got a new boyfriend," she whispered.

We walked down the hall to our room and waited for Miss Kerns to open the door. The boys were coming in from the boys' side. All of a sudden Dan ran over to me.

"Do you like marbles?" he asked in a low voice.

I nodded.

"Here." Without looking at me, he put something in my hand. It was a big aggie, white with red and yellow swirls and a blue stripe around the middle. Before I could say anything, he had disappeared into the room. When I came in and looked over at his desk, he was turned away, talking to the boy next to him.

Miss Kerns clapped her hands. "Time to get back to work. First we'll have a review of our multiplication tables to see how much you retained over the summer. We'll start with the twos. Bruce, why don't you begin."

I was so busy examining my new aggie and trying to see if Dan was looking at me that when Miss Kerns called on me for the sevens, at first I didn't hear her. Then I recited it so fast that I made a mistake and said seven times eight was fifty-five and had to write the correct answer on the blackboard ten times. It was embarrassing.

But at the same time secretly I was happy, too. Dan had given me the most beautiful marble I had ever seen. That had to mean he really liked me, just like Allie M had said. And even though I would never tell anybody, not even Allie M or even Martha, I really liked him, too.

After school Mimi's father picked her up to take her someplace so Danny and I walked home by ourselves. We walked slowly, being careful not to step on any of the lines on the sidewalk. *Step on a crack: break your mother's back. Step on a line: break your father's spine.* I had my hand in my pocket, rolling my aggie between my fingers, and remembering how Allie M had whispered that Dan was my boyfriend and then a minute later he had run over and given it to me.

Was he really my boyfriend? I had never had one before. In the second grade I had a crush on Francis Brown, mostly because of his blond curls, but he had never even noticed me. I used to walk behind him on the way home from school until I reached my street, just so I could look at his hair.

But now a boy liked me. It was funny that he was called Dan, almost like my brother, although his name was Dante, not Daniel. So now there were two Dans and two Allies who were really Alices. I wondered what kind of a name Dante was. I had never heard it before.

When we got home, my mother had made cocoa for us and there was a new box of animal crackers. Danny took all the elephants.

"Well, how was school?" she asked.

"Super!" Danny said. "Scott and Joey and I played with the trains and I was the conductor."

"That's wonderful," my mother said. "How about you, Allie?"

"Okay," I said.

"How is your teacher?"

"I think she's a little crabby."

"That's too bad. But you'll probably find out her bark is worse than her bite."

"That's exactly what Allie M said!"

While we had our snack, I told my mother all about Allie M and our names and how now at school I was Allie S. I didn't tell her about Dan or the aggie though. I decided not to tell anybody about that except Allie M, who already knew.

chapter
twenty-four

The next day Mimi and I walked to school together. I remembered how in the summer I had worried about walking with her, but it wasn't so bad after all. *Don't borrow trouble.* Now that I knew her better, I liked her quite a lot. And besides, I had already made some new friends in my class.

After school I was going to my first tap dancing class so I was carrying a bag with my tap shoes and Mrs. Greenberg's bloomers. My mother was really making me wear them. I had begged her not to, but she insisted that they were just the thing for dancing, since the legs had elastic and wouldn't ride up. And when I asked my father to make her change her mind, he wouldn't. He said the decision was up to her and that Mrs. Greenberg had made them especially for me and that I ought to be grateful.

At school Allie M had saved a place in line for me. While we were waiting to go in, I showed her the bloomers. She said she didn't think they looked so terrible, but I told her she hadn't seen them on.

When we went inside, I looked over at Dan and he smiled at me. Miss Kerns called the roll and then we all stood up and pledged allegiance and sang "The Star-Spangled Banner." At my old school, we had sung "My Country 'Tis of Thee." I couldn't reach the high notes at "the rocket's red glare," so I just moved my lips.

No matter how hard I tried, I couldn't forget about the bloomers. I tried to tell myself that maybe they weren't as stupid as I thought, but I knew that they were. Then I hoped that maybe some other girl would be wearing a pair, too, but I knew that was what my father called wishful thinking. I had never in my whole life ever seen anybody else wearing them except for babies.

After we finished singing, Miss Kerns called each one of us up to her desk to test our reading and divided us up into reading groups. Allie M and I were both in the Robins. Even though no one said so, I could tell the Robins were the best. The three other groups were the Crows, the Blue Jays, and the Chickadees. Dan was a Blue Jay. There were only three Chickadees and Allie M told me they were the worst. But Miss Kerns said the groups weren't carved in stone and that people might change their places as the year went on if they improved their reading skills.

For arithmetic we each got a brand-new workbook. We had to do the first three pages and then we passed them to the person next to us and Miss Kerns read off the answers and we marked them. I marked Tommy Rosa's and he got every one of them right. I got three wrong, two long division and one fraction.

By then it was time for lunch. Some kids, including Allie M and Dan, lived close enough to school to go home. The ones like me who had to stay all went to the gym to eat. I looked around, wondering where to sit. Everybody seemed to be sitting with somebody else. Finally I sat down by myself at an empty table in the corner. Just as I was thinking how embarrassing it felt not to have anybody to eat with, someone came over. It was one of the other girls in the Robins.

"Is it okay if I sit here?" she asked.

I nodded.

"I'm Sally May," she said.

I couldn't remember whether Sally May was her first name or her whole name but I felt funny asking her.

"I usually eat with Dolores but she's mad at me," she said. "It's because I'm in the Robins and she's not."

"What's she in?"

"The Crows."

"At my old school the reading groups had numbers," I said.

"Were you in one?"

"No, four. It went backward, but everybody knew four was the highest."

"Everybody knows here, too. Last year Dolores and I were both in the Zebras. They were the best. The Elephants came next, then the Tigers and then the Lions. There were only four Lions. They're the same as the Chickadees except one Lion stayed back."

I didn't ask who it was because I knew.

After lunch we went outside together. Sally May had a ball so we started playing "A My Name Is." When I got to G, I remembered what had happened the last time I played. This time I said graham crackers.

All afternoon, while we had geography and spelling and the music teacher came for singing, Dan and I kept peeking at each other. Then, when school was over and we were all lined up to go, he told Miss Kerns he had forgotten something in his desk. As he passed by me going back, he slipped a note into my hand. I looked around to see if anyone had noticed, but thank goodness everyone was busy talking and Miss Kerns was turned the other way.

Outside, as I started walking toward the community center, I read Dan's note. It had four words in it.

chapter twenty-five

YOU ARE VERY PRETTY

It said that! It really did! Dan thought I was very pretty! Yesterday he had given me his favorite aggie and today he had said I was very pretty!

I folded the note carefully and put it in my pocket. Then I took it out, unfolded it, and looked at it again. Each time I read it, I felt warm all over. No one had ever told me I was very pretty before except my grandmother, and she was a relative. And when my mother had said I was beautiful, it was just because of what Cynthia had called me. Movie stars like Shirley Temple and girls like Cynthia were really very pretty. But now someone not in my family thought I was, too!

All of a sudden it started to rain really hard. Little white hailstones bounced across the sidewalk like marbles. I ran as fast as I could, but by the time I got to the community center I was soaking wet. The man at the desk in the lobby pointed to the stairs.

"The gym's down there," he said.

Outside the gym a sign said: TAP DANCING — BEGINNER'S CLASS. As I opened the door, a tall lady in a ruffly red skirt came hurrying over.

"I'm Miss Herrara," she said. "You must be Alice Sherman. Everyone else is already here. Go into the locker room and put on your dance clothes before you catch your death of cold."

A bunch of girls were in the locker room changing. When I came in, they all stopped talking and looked at me. I didn't recognize any of them, but they all seemed to know each other. They were all wearing regular shorts and blouses.

I waited until they had all gone before I began to undress. My underpants were damp from the rain, but I was too embarrassed not to wear them, even if nobody could see. Slowly I pulled up the bloomers and wiggled into the sleeves. I sat on a bench and took off my shoes and socks. As I put on my new socks and my tap dance shoes, I started to shiver.

"Alice, we're about to begin!" Miss Herrara called in a loud voice.

I stood up. My wet underpants stuck to my skin as I walked

to the gym door. The class was facing the other way and at first only Miss Herrara saw me. She pointed to a place in the last row. My taps click-clacked on the shiny wooden floor and everybody turned around.

Then somebody said, "Ooh, bloomers!" and they all started to laugh.

I wanted to disappear.

"That's enough!" Miss Herrara said. She clapped her hands and told everybody to behave themselves.

Then the class started. First Miss Herrara had us sing "Three Blind Mice" and tap our toes to the rhythm. She showed us how to brush the front of our foot back and forth and move our weight from one foot to the other. She called it shuffling. It wasn't long before we had actually started tap dancing.

After that first minute nobody paid much attention to me again, not even Miss Herrara. But I couldn't concentrate on the dancing. I just kept shivering and thinking how stupid I looked. And despite what my mother had said, the bloomers were horrible to dance in. They stuck to my wet underpants and bunched up between my legs. I kept looking at the clock, counting the minutes until the class would be finished.

As soon as it was, I ran back to the locker room ahead of everyone else, grabbed my clothes, and raced out of the building.

As I passed the other girls, one of them said, "There goes the bloomer girl," and they all started laughing again.

The tap dancing shoes were hard to run in but I didn't care. I hurried down the stairs and onto the street. When I finally had to stop to catch my breath, I hid behind some bushes and pulled my dress on over the bloomers. Then I sat down and changed my shoes and slowly walked the rest of the way home.

I never wanted to see that place again. I hated the class. I hated the nasty girls. I hated my mother for making me wear the stupid bloomers. I hated Mrs. Greenberg for making them in the first place.

I started to pray. Dear God, I whispered. Please make something happen so I don't have to go back there anymore. If You do, I promise to always be nice to Danny and be a good girl for ever and ever.

My mother was in the kitchen with Danny, playing Chinese checkers.

"How was the tap dancing?" she asked. "Was it fun?"

"It was horrible," I said. "I'm not going anymore."

"Don't be silly!" she said in an annoyed voice. "You've been looking forward to it all year. Anyway, we bought you your new shoes and I've already paid for all the classes."

I started to shiver again. "I don't feel good," I said.

My mother pressed her lips against my forehead.

"You *are* warm," she said, looking worried. "I hope you're not coming down with something."

But I hoped I was.

chapter twenty-six

God answered my prayers. I got the measles. I had asked Him for help and He had been listening. And He answered so fast. I thought it was pretty funny that He had given me spots all over. It was as if the polka dots on the bloomers had given Him the idea. Of course I didn't tell anybody. They wouldn't have believed me anyway.

I was pretty sick for a few days. I had a high temperature, my head ached, and the light hurt my eyes. My mother kept putting cold compresses on my forehead. She made me chicken soup with noodles and she cut the crusts off the toast, the way she always did when we were sick. And she brought all my meals up on the fancy yellow and blue tray she'd gotten for a wedding present.

When I was feeling a little bit better, I was allowed to have visitors, but only people who had already had the measles so they were immune and wouldn't catch it from me. Martha hadn't had them yet, but Claire had, so she came over one afternoon and helped me cut out a new book of paper dolls she and Martha had bought for me as a get-well present. And even though she had always said paper dolls were babyish, she played with me until suppertime, we were having so much fun. But she told me something that really bothered me. She said Martha had started playing with Cynthia again. Mimi came over a few times, too. She had had the measles already. She had already had almost everything.

By the time I was all better, I had missed too many tap dancing lessons to catch up, so Miss Herrara gave us back our money. My mother said she would try to sell the shoes at the next Temple Sisterhood rummage sale. At first I was a little sad when I thought that now I would probably never learn to tap dance. But when I remembered that girl's voice saying, "Ooh, bloomers!" and the whole class laughing at me, I didn't care.

On my first day back at school, Allie M was waiting for me in line. She gave me a hug and said she was really glad to see me. When we got to our room, Dan looked up from his desk and gave me a little wave. Then Miss Kerns came over to me.

"Welcome back," she said, shaking my hand. "You've got a lot of catching up to do."

Today it was Dan's turn to call the roll. When he got to my name, his face turned red.

"Allie Sh . . . Sh . . . Sherman," he said, stuttering. A few kids laughed.

Miss Kerns clapped her hands. "Rule Number Two!" she said in a warning voice.

After school Mimi and I walked home together. I told her I'd meet her in the morning. I knew she had hoped I would ask her over to play. But I didn't. I really wanted to see Martha by myself that afternoon.

As soon as I had changed into my play clothes, I went next door and called for her. When she came out, I told her I had something important to ask her.

"What?"

I took a deep breath. "Claire said you've been going over to Cynthia's house after school."

"Oh, just once in a while."

When I didn't say anything, Martha said, "Well, while you had the measles, I didn't have anyone else to play with."

I swallowed hard. "Then is Cynthia your best friend again?"

Martha looked uncomfortable. "Only sometimes," she said. "We're best friends at school, but you're my best friend at home."

I said that didn't make sense. You couldn't have two best friends at the same time, even if they were in different places. But Martha said you could. She explained that since she and Cynthia were in the same class, it felt funny not to talk to each other, so they had made up.

"What about Cynthia's father?" I asked. "I thought he wouldn't let her come over to your house anymore?"

"He won't," she said. "But I can go there. That's why we're only best friends at school and you and I can still be best friends at home. Anyway, what does it matter? You and I don't go to school together anyway."

"But you're my best friend all the time, even when I'm at school," I said. "Besides, what if Cynthia's father decides to let her come over again? What about that?"

She didn't answer.

I persisted. "Who would be your best friend here if Cynthia could come over again?"

When she still didn't answer, I said I had to do my homework and went inside.

Danny was playing cars in the upstairs hall.

"Did you and Martha have a fight?" he asked.

It was almost as if he was a mind reader sometimes.

"I bet it was about Cynthia."

I surprised myself by telling him what had happened.

"Why don't you get another best friend?" he asked.

I had never thought of that before. I had been so happy that Martha had asked me to be her best friend that it had never occurred to me that I had anything to say about it.

"Mimi could be your best friend."

"Don't be stupid!"

"Well, why not? She's funner to play with than Martha."

I went up to my room and threw myself onto my bed. The little balls on my chenille bedspread felt bumpy against my face. What should I do? It wasn't fair for Martha to just decide by herself that I was only her best friend sometimes. But what was even worse was that she didn't seem to see anything wrong with it. And even though I knew Cynthia hadn't done anything to her, it still made me feel funny that Martha could still like her after what she had said to me.

chapter twenty-seven

It was the first day of Hanukkah and three days before Christmas. This year they overlapped. In our family we celebrated Christmas, too, even though we were Jewish. My parents divided the two holidays. My mother did everything for Hanukkah and my father did everything for Christmas. I used to think it was Santa Claus that did Christmas but now I thought it was my father. Danny still thought it was Santa Claus.

Sometime I felt a little funny celebrating Christmas because most Jewish people didn't. But I loved it so much that I couldn't imagine not having it. And besides, it was the birthday of Jesus Christ, and now that I knew he was Jewish it felt kind of okay, even though we didn't believe he was the son of God.

Mimi had been surprised that we celebrated Christmas. Her family didn't. But they didn't celebrate Hanukkah either. She said they did when her grandparents were alive but now that they were dead they didn't anymore. I really felt sorry for her.

In a way we only half-celebrated Christmas because we didn't have a Christmas tree. My mother said she drew the line at that. We didn't put a wreath on our door either. And our relatives didn't give us Christmas presents. So it wasn't the way Martha and her family celebrated.

But it was my very favorite holiday of the whole year, even without a tree or a wreath. It was so exciting. First you made a list of all the things you wanted and then you wrote a letter to Santa Claus and then on Christmas Eve you left Santa Claus milk and cookies and the next morning you got up so early that it was still dark and you waited until they said you could go into the living room and there was a big pile of presents and your stocking was all full and the milk and cookies were gone.

Hanukkah wasn't as exciting as Christmas but it lasted for a longer time. You got eight presents, one for each night, but they were only little ones, like crayons or jacks, except on the first night when we each got a book. And it was fun to light the candles on the menorah every night and sing "Rock of Ages." After that we played games with a top that was called a *dreidel* and got Hanukkah *gelt*, which was chocolate coins wrapped in gold paper. My father loved the potato pancakes and applesauce that my mother made for supper on the first and last nights. She only made them on Hanukkah. She said it was traditional to just have them on the holiday because it made them special. Besides, they were a lot of work.

This year I had gotten *Heidi Grows Up*, which I had really wanted. I had borrowed it from the library but that wasn't the same thing as owning it. When you owned a book, you could write your name in it and read it again and again whenever you wanted to and you never had to return it.

Before supper my mother got the menorah out of the dining room cabinet. My grandma had brought it over with her from Russia a long time ago, and when she had died she left it to my mother. My mother remembered polishing it when she was a little girl and now it was my job. It was made out of brass and I had polished it until it was as shiny as gold.

My mother lit a candle and handed it to me. I used it to light the first candle in the menorah and then I put it in the middle place. Each night for eight days you lit one more candle until on the eighth night the menorah was completely full. The reason you did this was to remember what happened to the Jews thousands of years ago when Judas Maccabee and his four brothers fought against the Syrians and drove them out of Israel and got back the Temple in Jerusalem.

Then they had to clean the Temple and relight the eternal light, which they were supposed to never allow to go out.

But even though they only had enough oil for one night, the lamp burned for eight nights, which was a miracle. So on Hanukkah you lit candles for eight nights to remember what had happened long ago.

chapter twenty-eight

One day after school Allie M walked home with me and Danny. It was the first time she had come over to play. When we got to our house, she said it was beautiful.

I had never thought of our house as beautiful. To me it just looked like a regular house. I thought some of the other houses on our block were prettier and some of them were bigger, too. But Allie M said she liked ours best.

I knew that she and her mother lived on the second floor of a two-family house, sort of like our apartment at the Greenbergs'. And I knew they rented one of their bedrooms to a boarder, to make money. But Allie M had never invited me over.

It was a really sunny day, so we decided to have our snack outside and turn it into a tea party with some of my dolls. My mother poured our chocolate milk into a tea-pot. And instead of glasses she let us use cups and saucers, the ones that she and my father used for their coffee. We put everything on a tray and carried it out to the front stoop.

I had given Allie M first dibs on choosing a doll because she was my guest. She picked Jane and I picked Honeybunch. We sat them down next to us on the steps and poured out milk for everyone. Then we helped ourselves to the Lorna Doones. My mother had put eight of them on a plate, because there were four of us, including the dolls. But we could eat their cookies, too.

I had already finished two of mine and was reaching for another one when I noticed that Allie M was still on her first. She was nibbling it very slowly and whenever a crumb fell, she picked it up and ate it.

"Do you have cookies every day after school?" she asked me.

I nodded. "But usually only graham crackers. But today is special because you're a guest." I looked at her. "Don't you?"

"What?"

"Have cookies after school?"

She shook her head. "They cost too much," she said.

"What do you have?"

"Bread and grape jelly, mostly," she said. She looked a little embarrassed.

"That's good, too," I said.

I poured us each some more milk and we gave more to our dolls.

"Jane really likes this chocolate milk!" Allie M said.

"She's never had it before," I said. "Neither has Honeybunch. She only has water."

Just then I noticed the Bryants' car pull up in their driveway. It was a Monday, so Martha was coming home from catechism. When she got out of the car, I waved to her.

Martha went into her house. I figured she would change into her play clothes and then come over. I told Allie M about her and how she was Catholic and went to St. John's.

"I used to go to St. John's, too," Allie M said.

"You never told me that," I said. "Did you know Martha?"

She shook her head. "I was only there for kindergarten. She must have been in the other class. But when my father went away, we couldn't afford it anymore. Anyway, I like Center School better. The nuns were really strict."

"That's what Martha says," I said. "Did you know Cynthia Conners?"

Allie M nodded and made a face. "She was in my class. She used to make fun of everyone. Do you know her?"

"She's Martha's . . . she's a good friend of Martha's."

"Well, maybe she's changed," Allie M said.

I told her she'd gotten worse.

We gave the dolls some more to eat and then took them for a walk up and down the front path in their carriage. I kept looking over at Martha's house but she didn't come out. Finally Allie M said she had to go home. I said I'd walk her to the corner. That way I could keep an eye out for the neighborhood bully, Sonny Marco, in case he tried to bother her. But luckily he wasn't around.

On the way back Martha was waiting for me on the sidewalk.

"Who was that?" she asked.

"Allie M," I said. "Remember I told you she was in my class?"

"I didn't know you played with her after school."

"Today was the first time she came over. We had the best tea party!"

"Will she come over again?" Martha asked.

"I hope so," I said. "We really had fun!"

Martha didn't say anything.

"Do you want to play tea party some more?" I asked. "There's still some chocolate milk left."

Martha shook her head. "I've got a lot of homework," she said. "Anyway, I think tea parties are sort of babyish, don't you?"

I didn't answer. I'd never thought about it before. All I knew was that I loved them, babyish or not. And up until now Martha had, too. I wondered if Claire had said something to her.

And then, just as she was turning to go inside, I suddenly knew what the matter was. It wasn't Claire and it wasn't that tea parties were babyish either.

Martha was jealous!

chapter twenty-nine

It was a Sunday morning early in March when I noticed these pretty little white flowers blooming along the driveway.

"They're snowdrops," my mother said when I took her out to look at them. "We used to have them in our yard when I was a little girl. That means it's almost spring."

And then it started to snow.

"Well, you know the saying," she said. "March comes in like a lion and goes out like a lamb."

At first there were just a few flakes but then all of a sudden they were falling so hard that you couldn't see out the window. We turned on the radio and it said we were having a blizzard.

Danny and I put on our snowsuits and galoshes and went outside. The treetops were rocking wildly back and forth and the wind was howling. The snowflakes swirled around us, clinging to our clothes and turning us into living snowmen.

We tried to build a real snowman, but the snow wasn't sticky enough. So we just chased each other around the yard and made snow angels.

By the next morning there was over three feet of snow and school was called off. The first Snow Day of the whole year! The sun was shining and the sky was bright blue. Today the snow was perfect for snowmen. Martha came over and we got to work. We had finished one and were almost done with the second when we saw Mimi crossing the street. She asked us if we wanted to build an igloo in her yard.

Danny said okay. He always agreed to anything Mimi suggested. But Martha and I weren't sure. We were having so much fun making our snow family.

"I've never built an igloo before," I said.

"Neither have I," said Martha.

"I'll show you how," Mimi said. "I built one last year with my father."

We still weren't sure.

"It can be our clubhouse," she said. "And we can pretend to be Eskimos."

That sounded good. I looked at Martha and she nodded.

"All right," I said. "But first we want to finish our snow-woman."

We tied an old scarf of my mother's on her head and a checkered apron around her middle. Our snowman was smoking a bubble pipe and wearing Danny's cowboy hat. They really looked funny together.

We all walked across the street to Mimi's front yard. I could tell that she was really excited to have Martha playing over at her house. In all the time I'd known them, this was the first time it had happened.

To build an igloo, first you made a whole lot of blocks of snow. Then you drew a big circle in the snow, the size you wanted for your igloo, and set the blocks on it, leaving an opening for a door. After that, you kept on making more snow blocks and piling them up in layers like bricks, putting each block halfway and a little bit over the edge of the two blocks under it so that the wall curved inward.

Mimi was the boss because she was the only one who had ever built an igloo before. Martha remembered seeing it.

"I thought it was so neat!" she said.

"You should have come over," Mimi said.

Martha didn't answer, but we all knew that back then she hardly even spoke to Mimi.

"After a few days the walls got just like ice," Mimi said. "The floor, too. We brought an old rug out and some pillows to sit on. And we toasted marshmallows."

Danny's eyes were wide as saucers. "With a fire?"

"With a Sterno stove."

"What's that?" Martha asked.

"It's this little stove with a can with stuff in it that burns and you can cook on it. My father bought it."

"Do you think he'll let us use it?" Danny asked.

"Maybe," she said.

I could tell she was embarrassed because her father didn't live there anymore.

"If we don't get busy, we won't have an igloo to cook in," I said.

At that everyone got to work again making snow blocks. But by the time it started getting dark, we had still only built up four layers.

"Maybe we made it too big around," Martha said.

"We couldn't all fit inside if we made it any smaller," I answered.

"I'm freezing," Danny said.

"Do you want to come in for cocoa?" Mimi asked.

Danny nodded and looked at me. I hesitated, thinking about Mrs. Minnick. Martha didn't answer either.

When no one said anything, Danny tugged at my sleeve impatiently.

"Okay," I said finally. I felt uncomfortable because I could tell Mimi knew what I had been thinking. "Cocoa would be great."

All of us looked at Martha. When she nodded in agreement, we all followed Mimi around to her back porch. We took off our galoshes and went into the kitchen.

Mrs. Minnick was sitting at the kitchen table as usual, smoking and drinking a cup of coffee. The radio was on. *Stella Dallas.*

"We've come in to have cocoa," Mimi announced. "I can make it."

"I don't think there's any milk," Mrs. Minnick said. "But you can use water."

We all stood there while Mimi went into the pantry. She came out with a tin of cocoa and a box of marshmallows.

"Where did you find those?" her mother asked her. "I didn't know we had any left."

"I hid them," Mimi said.

"Aren't you the clever puss?" her mother said in that sarcastic way I hated. She looked over at Martha. "Well, this is an honor."

Martha smiled uncertainly.

Mrs. Minnick turned to me. "And how are you, Allie?"

I told her I was fine.

"I'm fine, too," Danny said.

Suddenly Mrs. Minnick sneezed. "KERCHOO!"

It was the biggest, noisiest sneeze I had ever heard. Her face turned bright red and her whole body shook.

"God bless you!" Danny and I said together.

"Thank you," she said, wiping her eyes and nose with the corner of her apron. Then she sneezed again, even louder, and she started laughing. "If there's anything that feels better than a good sneeze, I don't know what it is."

She turned to Mimi. "I think I'll have some of that cocoa, too," she said. "I must be catching a cold."

Mimi carefully poured out five cups of cocoa. Even though they didn't all match, the cups and saucers were beautiful. When I said how pretty they were, Mrs. Minnick said they had been her mother's in Russia.

"Just like ours!" Danny said. "Only we only have three."

"Well, we only have three that match, too," Mrs. Minnick said. "The rest of the set are broken. But I always say, if you can't use your beautiful things, what's the use of having them?"

As I sipped my cocoa, which was sort of watery, I thought about how we never were allowed to use my grandmother's dishes. They just sat in the dining room cabinet like decorations. As for the sneezing, I had never thought about how a sneeze felt before. But now that I did, I sort of knew what Mrs. Minnick meant.

When we'd finished our cocoa, we got ready to go. Mimi followed us out to the back porch.

"You'll come back tomorrow to work on the igloo, won't you?" she asked.

We all promised we would.

When we got home, I went into the dining room and stared at my grandmother's cups and saucers. My mother had said that someday they would be mine. I wondered whether when I grew up I would let my little girl drink from them like Mrs. Minnick or be like my mother and keep them safe behind glass doors.

chapter thirty

The next day we went over to Mimi's right after breakfast and got back to work on our igloo. Mimi had decided that three people would make the blocks while the fourth person built up the wall. That made the work go faster and by lunchtime we were nearly done.

Only a few more short rows were left to do before the whole igloo would be finished, but then we ran into a problem. None of us could reach high enough to put the last blocks in place and close the hole in the roof. We stood around wondering what to do.

"We could leave the hole and pretend it's sort of a chimney," Danny suggested.

"That way we'd have more light," Martha said.

"Like a window in the ceiling," I said.

But Mimi said that then it wouldn't be a real igloo.

Finally we decided we needed a stepladder. Mimi got one and Martha stood up on top of it because she was the tallest, and we handed her snow blocks. She placed them neatly side by side, smoothing the edges so that they all fit together perfectly. In a little while the igloo was completely finished.

We all stood back to admire it. It looked just like the pictures of igloos you saw in books and magazines; the only thing that was different was that there weren't any Eskimos in fur parkas posing in front.

"I wish we could take a picture of it," Mimi said. "Does anyone have a camera?"

"We do!" Danny said. He ran across the street and in a little while he came back with our mother. For the first picture, she had us all line up in front of the igloo. Then we all wiggled inside it and stuck our heads out the door for another one.

That was the last Snow Day we had all winter. But from then on every day right after school, we would meet in our igloo and play. We furnished it with all kinds of stuff. Mimi supplied a rug and some pillows. Martha brought an old patchwork quilt and a book called *The Eskimo Twins.* Danny and I contributed some chipped cups and a tin pot. And Mrs. Minnick found the Sterno stove for us. Each day we would light it and melt snow in the pot for cocoa. Even though it was watery, it really tasted good.

And then we would toast marshmallows. We pretended that the marshmallows were blubber and that we were the family from *The Eskimo Twins.* Danny was Menie, the boy twin, and Mimi was Monnie, the girl. Martha and I took turns being the father because we didn't have any more boys. The mother's name was Koolee and the father's was Kesshoo. The book said that if you said it fast, it sounded just like a sneeze. When I told Mrs. Minnick about that, she laughed.

But after a while the weather got warmer and our igloo started to melt. Finally all that was left was a pile of slushy snow. But my mother had given everybody copies of the pictures she had taken for souvenirs.

And pretty soon it was really spring.

chapter thirty-one

A few nights later after supper we heard a familiar bell ringing.

"The Good Humor man!" I yelled. "He's back!"

My mother gave us each a nickel for popsicles and we ran outside. Martha and Claire were just coming out of their house so we all walked up to the corner together.

Martha and Claire had dimes. Danny and I hardly ever got dime Good Humors. At the corner we found Mimi waiting in line with her father.

"Well, look who's here!" Mr. Minnick said with a big smile. He was all dressed up as usual in a navy blue suit and a tie and shiny black shoes. "If it isn't Allie and Martha and Claire! And who is this little fellow?"

Danny scowled. He hated being called little.

"He's my brother," I said. "Danny."

"Well, how do you do, Danny," said Mr. Minnick, putting out his hand. "I'm glad to finally meet you. You've got a very nice big sister."

Danny stuck his hands in his pockets. I poked him.

"That's all right," Mr. Minnick said. "I never liked to shake hands either when I was his age. What are you kids having?"

We told him.

"Are you sure you wouldn't rather have ice cream?" he asked Danny and me. "It's my treat."

Danny's face lit up. "Could I have chocolate?" he asked.

By then it was Mr. Minnick's turn in line. He bought six Good Humors: a strawberry for Mimi, two chocolates for him and Danny, creamsicles for Claire and Martha, and a coconut for me. I loved coconut.

We all started walking back together. When we got to Martha and Claire's house, Mr. Minnick said good-bye. We all thanked him again for treating us and sat down on the stoop.

"Now we can get ten-cent Good Humors next time, too, because we still have our nickels," Danny said to me. He turned to Mimi. "Your father must be rich."

Just then we heard our mother's whistle, which meant it was time to go home.

"Tell Mommy I'll be there in a minute," I said to Danny. "I just have to finish my ice cream."

I licked the last bit slowly to make it last longer. After I had licked the stick clean, I closed my eyes and recited my special magic charm before looking at it: *Fee fie fo fum. Let the free stick quickly come.* Then I opened my eyes and looked down.

I let out a shriek. It was a free stick! I had never gotten one before! They only came with ten-cent Good Humors.

"Lucky Haras," Martha whispered to me.

"Maybe you'll get one next time, Neleh," I whispered back.

"What did you and Martha just whisper to each other?" Mimi asked.

I answered without thinking. "None of your beeswax!"

Martha and Claire giggled.

Mimi stared at me, but I didn't say anything. After a minute she stood up and walked away.

"See you tomorrow," I called after her.

She turned around. Her face had that old crybaby look. "No, you won't," she said. "And that free stick isn't really yours anyway. My father paid for it."

She ran across the street and went home.

chapter thirty-two

That night I had a hard time falling asleep. I kept thinking about what had happened at Martha's with Mimi and how mean I had been to her. But then I would think about what Mimi had said, about the free stick really not being mine, and how mean that was, too. And it all kept bouncing back and forth in my mind until I couldn't stand it anymore. It really wasn't any of her business if Martha and I were best friends. Which we still were except when Martha was at school.

Anyway, what was I supposed to do? I couldn't help it if I liked Martha better. Besides, even if I ever did like Mimi the same, it wouldn't matter because I didn't like her family. Even when she was friendly, Mrs. Minnick always made me feel as if underneath she was making fun of me. And Mr. Minnick, even though he had treated us to ice cream, was always a little scary, all dressed up and fancy all the time and always smiling, even when there was nothing to smile about.

When I woke up the next morning, Mimi was the first thing I thought about. So I decided that after breakfast I would go call for her and make friends again. I let Danny come with me.

But when I knocked on Mimi's back door, no one answered.

"She's not home," Danny said.

"But she's got to be. It's so early and besides, she hardly ever goes anywhere."

"Maybe she's still sleeping."

"She never sleeps this late," I said. I walked down from the porch and yelled her name. Mrs. Minnick stuck her head out of an upstairs window. She looked cross.

"What do you want?" she asked.

"Can Mimi come out and play?"

"She's not feeling well."

Without another word, she shut the window. Danny and I walked back down the driveway.

"I bet she really isn't sick," I said. "I bet she's lying."

Danny looked surprised. "Why would she lie?"

I told him what had happened last night after he went home. Not our secret names though.

"Why can't you and Martha be best friends with Mimi, too?" he asked.

"Don't be silly. Three people can't be best friends."

"Why not?"

"They just can't be. Besides, I don't want to be best friends with her."

Danny didn't answer. We walked together side by side across the street and up our driveway. Our footsteps matched, left, right, left, right, like soldiers. At our back door, just before we went inside, he turned to me.

"You think Martha is so great," he said. "But I think Mimi is more . . . ," he paused, trying to think of just the right word, "more *interesting*."

chapter thirty-three

The phone rang. My mother answered it.

"That was Mrs. Minnick," she said when she hung up. "The doctor just came. Mimi has scarlet fever. They're under quarantine."

She explained that quarantine meant that nobody could go in or out of their house except the nurse and doctor. It was because scarlet fever was very contagious. Contagious meant that anybody who went near her could catch it. And sure enough, when we looked outside, we saw a man putting up a sign on their front door. It was yellowish-brown and it said in big letters:

SCARLET FEVER
THESE PREMISES ARE UNDER QUARANTINE

I knew that scarlet fever was really serious. Beth in *Little Women* had almost died from it. Was Mimi going to die?

"I'm sure she'll get better," my mother said. "She's a big strong girl." But she had a worried look on her face.

I could write her letters, my mother said, even though she couldn't write back. And I could talk to her on the telephone, but not for a few days because she was still so weak.

"What about school?" I asked.

"Her teacher will send her some lessons to do at home," my mother said. "But she won't be able to send any of her work back because there might be germs on it."

"You mean you can catch scarlet fever from paper?"

"From anything the sick person touches," my mother said. "After she's better, they'll have to burn all her bedclothes and pajamas and the toys she's played with."

Burn her toys? Poor Mimi. And my mother said that her father couldn't even come to see her, because then he couldn't leave the house again to go to work. When Martha came over, I told her about Mimi. She couldn't believe about the burning.

"I couldn't stand it if they burned Beverly Jane," Martha said. Beverly Jane was her favorite doll. She had real hair.

"I couldn't stand it if they burned Shirley. Or Oliver or Brenda." I tried to remember if Mimi had any dolls. I had never been in her bedroom and she had never brought any over. But she did have some favorite paper dolls and a stuffed monkey named Perky that she had told me she slept with.

We went up to my room and we wrote her a letter together.

Dear Mimi,

We're sorry you got scarlet fever. We hope it doesn't hurt too much. In a few days we'll call you on the telephone. We hope you get better soon.

Your friends,
Allie and Martha

"Should we say anything about what happened?" I asked Martha.

"What should we say?" she asked.

We thought for a while and finally decided on something:

P.S. It wasn't nice of us to whisper in front of you and for Allie to say none of your beeswax, and we're sorry. We won't do it anymore.

We put the letter in an envelope and wrote Mimi's name on the front. Then we went downstairs to find my mother.

She said she would give us a stamp and we could go put it in the mailbox at the corner. She thought that was better than bringing it over to Mimi's house, even if we just left it on the porch. You never know, she said.

When we walked to the corner, Sonny Marco was in his front yard shooting marbles. As usual he stuck out his tongue.

"Just ignore him, Haras," Martha whispered to me, taking my hand and walking faster.

"All right, Neleh," I whispered back.

We got to the mailbox and put our letter in the slot. It seemed kind of funny to mail a letter to someone who lived right across the street.

"Do you think it was my fault?" I asked Martha as we were walking back.

"You mean about Mimi getting scarlet fever?"

I nodded.

"How could it be?" Martha asked. "You don't have it so how could you give it to her?"

I didn't answer. It was just the way things had happened, with us being mean to Mimi and then her getting sick and my thinking she was lying when she really wasn't and then her getting scarlet fever, which some people died from.

"Well?" Martha said.

"I don't know. I just feel funny."

"I know," she said. She kicked a stone.

We walked along slowly.

"From now on we'll have to be really nice to her," I said. I kicked the stone.

Martha nodded. "We could send her a get-well present."

"She'll have to burn it when she gets better," I said.

"Not if it's something to eat. We could bake her some cookies."

Martha kicked the stone really far. It landed in front of her driveway. When we got there, she said she had to go do her homework. But first we decided that we would bake Toll House cookies as soon as we could. We decided to bake them at her house because her mother always let her and Claire bake when they wanted to. I said I'd ask my mother to buy us the chocolate chips.

chapter thirty-four

Since Mimi had gotten sick, my mother had been calling Mrs. Minnick every day to find out how she was. And up until now there had not been any change. Mimi was still really sick. But then one day when I got home after school, my mother told me that the doctor had just been to see Mimi and that she was going to be all right.

"Thank God!" my mother said. "What that poor woman has been going through."

"Was she afraid Mimi would die?" I asked.

"Mimi was very sick," my mother said. "Mr. and Mrs. Minnick were terribly worried."

She said I could call Mimi up. Mimi answered the phone herself. She said she had gotten our letter and our cookies and that we could be friends again and that she was contagious for two more weeks.

When I asked her what she did all day, she said not much. Sometimes she listened to the radio or played with her paper dolls. I asked her if she read stories. She said she didn't because it hurt her eyes. I thought to myself that it was probably also because she didn't read very well, but of course I didn't say that.

"How about your mother? Does she read to you?"

"Sometimes. Not much."

All of a sudden I had an idea.

"What if I read to you? Over the telephone. Would you like that?"

"Oh, yes!" she said in an excited voice. Then she added doubtfully, "Will you really do it?"

"I'll have to ask my mother if it's okay," I said. "But if she says yes, I really will."

My mother said it was a good idea as long as I didn't stay on the phone more than half an hour. I called Mimi back and asked her what book she'd like me to read. She said I should choose one.

Up in my room I went through my books one by one, trying to decide which would be best. Would she like a fairy tale? I loved fairy tales, but some of them were pretty scary, like "Bluebeard" and "Beauty and the Beast." Maybe *Heidi*. That was the book we had read one day when we were playing school, but it might be more fun to start with something new. *Little Women* was wonderful, but parts of it were really sad, especially about Beth. Then I remembered *Mary Poppins*.

It was one of my most favorites. And I decided it would really cheer Mimi up.

When I called her back and told her the book I had chosen, she said she'd never heard of it. She told me to hold on a minute while she got comfortable. I put the book on the kitchen table and sat down, facing the clock. It was exactly three thirty. Martha would be home at four. I held the receiver to my ear with my right hand and turned the pages with my left. Then I began to read.

I loved the beginning, about asking the policeman at the crossroads how to find Cherry-Tree Lane and his funny directions. Then I went on to the next paragraph, where you get there.

Suddenly I stopped reading.

"Well, go on!" Mimi said impatiently.

I had stopped because a new thought had popped into my head. In all the times I had read *Mary Poppins,* I had never once connected Cherry-Tree Lane and Strawberry Hill until now. Maybe it was because I had never said Cherry-Tree Lane out loud before. But I had always loved that the cherry trees went dancing right down the middle of Cherry-Tree Lane and so I had expected that the strawberries would be dancing down the hill on Strawberry Hill, too. And when they weren't . . .

"Are you still there?" Mimi asked impatiently. "Why did you stop?"

I apologized and told her what I had been thinking about.

She didn't say anything.

Now it was my turn to ask if she was still there.

"I was just thinking," she said finally.

"What about?"

"Oh, nothing," she said vaguely. Her voice sounded strange.

"Are you okay?" I asked.

"I'm fine," she said. "Aren't you going to keep reading?"

I looked up at the clock. It was almost four. I told her I had to get off the phone.

"I'm sorry we didn't get very far," I said. "But don't worry. Tomorrow I'll read the whole time."

After I hung up, I picked up *Mary Poppins* and stared at the pinky-red cover. It almost matched my bedspread. I wondered if the cover was that color because of the cherry trees.

All of a sudden I had an idea. I emptied out my piggy bank and counted the money. One dollar and sixteen cents. I went downstairs to find my mother and tell her what I had thought of. She thought it was a good idea, too.

chapter thirty-five

On Mondays Martha had catechism lessons and got home late, so I had told Mimi I would call her right after school. By now we had reached the fifth chapter of *Mary Poppins,* the one that starts with Jane being in bed with an earache.

But when I called, Mimi said she had already read that chapter.

"How did you do that?" I asked, acting as if I was really surprised.

"I have my own book!" she said in an excited voice. "Somebody left it on the porch last night! They rang the doorbell, but when my mother answered it no one was there. But there was a package, all wrapped up in beautiful pink paper with silver ribbon! And on the outside was a card with my name on it!"

"Who was it from?"

"We don't know! It wasn't signed. But you want to know the funniest thing of all? It's a cow card!"

"What's so funny about that?" I asked.

"Don't you remember? Chapter Five is called 'The Dancing Cow.' And on the card someone drew a picture of a cow jumping over the moon on the front and inside they wrote:

Hey diddle diddle, the cat and the fiddle,
The cow jumped over the moon.
The little dog laughed to see such sport
And he hopes you are better real soon.

Isn't that weird?"

"It sure is," I said. "Do you have any idea who sent it?"

"We thought it was probably my father. He's the only one besides us who knows I'm reading *Mary Poppins.* But when I called him, he said it wasn't him."

"He's probably fibbing," I said.

"I don't think so," Mimi said. "He really sounded surprised. But who else could it be?"

I didn't say anything.

All of a sudden Mimi burst out laughing. "It's you, isn't it?" she said. "Come on, tell the truth!"

Finally I admitted it. "I thought it would be fun if you

could follow along while I was reading," I said. "Or sometimes you could read, too, just like you did when we were playing school. Would you like that?"

"I'd love it!" Mimi said. "And you know something else? It's the most wonderful present I've ever gotten in my whole life!"

"Oh, Mimi, come on!" I said. "You must have gotten nicer presents than that."

"This was the best," she insisted. "The way it was wrapped and the surprise and the mystery and the cow card and . . ." she paused, then burst out, ". . . and that it was you who gave it to me! That was the best of all!"

"My mother helped pay for it," I told her. "I didn't have quite enough money in my piggy bank so she gave me the rest. And she wrapped it. So it's really from her, too."

"Your mother is so nice," Mimi said. "Tell her thank you."

I mumbled something, feeling a little surprised at what she had said. I never really thought of my mother as being especially nice. I mean, I thought she was all right and I loved her, but if I thought about her being nice, it was mostly being nice to Danny, not to me. I thought Mrs. Bryant was nice because she never scolded Martha or Claire or had fights with Mr. Bryant.

We decided that Mimi would read the whole chapter out loud to me, now that she had practiced. We only had time for the first two pages today, but she did a really good job. Even though she went pretty slow and she missed a few words like "earache" and "gizzard" and "extraordinary," she read all the rest almost perfectly. When I told her how much she had improved, she was really proud.

chapter thirty-six

When I hung up the phone, I went to find my mother and Danny, who had both been in on the secret.

"Did she guess it was you?" Danny asked.

"Not right away," I said. "At first she thought it was her father, but she finally figured it out. She said it was the best present she had ever gotten!" I turned to my mother. "And she said I should tell you that you were really nice to help pay for it and wrap it."

"Well, thank you!" my mother said, looking pleased. "But it was your idea."

"And it wasn't even her birthday!" Danny said.

I went up to my room and shut the door. I wanted to be by myself for a while. I took my aggie out from its secret place and rolled it around in my hand. I did that a lot. I sort of thought of it as my good-luck charm.

When I had first gotten it, I had tried to figure out where

to keep it. I was afraid that if I put it in my jewelry box, Danny would find it. I knew he snooped in my things sometimes, even though he said he didn't. I could hide it under my underwear or blouses in one of my bureau drawers, but then my mother might come across it when she was putting away my clean clothes.

Finally I had decided to put it under my mattress, just like "The Princess and the Pea." Afterward I had lain down on my bed to see if I could feel it, but I couldn't because I wasn't a princess.

In the late afternoon the sun came through my window. I loved to hold my aggie up to the light and turn it around so that it made colored sparkles on the wall. I had laughed at Mimi when she said that *Mary Poppins* was the best present she had ever gotten, but in a way I thought that my aggie was the best present I had ever gotten, and an aggie was even smaller than a book and didn't cost as much either.

Just then Danny came in without even knocking. I was about to get mad at him, when he held out his hand with a letter in it.

"This just came in the mail for you," he said, all excited. "I think it's from Ruthie."

I took the letter with my left hand because I was hiding the aggie in my right one, but luckily he didn't notice.

"Well, aren't you going to open it?" he asked.

"Later," I said. You can't open a letter with one hand.

"But don't you want to know what she says?"

"Oh, she's probably just telling me about school and boring stuff like that. Besides, I was just going to start my homework."

When he didn't leave, I told him I wanted to do my homework in private.

"I'll be really quiet," he said. He didn't want to go because he wanted to know what was in the letter. My father said that Danny was very curious, which was a very good attribute, but I just thought he was nosy.

"Get out," I said. "Please."

When he left, I opened Ruthie's letter. She had written it on a piece of lined paper with two holes punched in it, the kind in school notebooks. She had printed it because she wasn't very good at script.

Dear Allie,

I'm sorry I didn't write before to thank you for the Indian bracelet. It's really pretty but sometimes it leaves black marks on my wrist. Did it do that on yours? My mother was glad you liked the bloomers. How do you like your new school?

I have Mrs. Tolando, but she's going to have a baby and she's really fat so they have to get a new teacher.

Your friend,

Ruthie

P.S. Please write back soon.

I read the letter three times, thinking about everything in it, which wasn't much. I didn't remember the bracelet making black marks on my wrist. I remembered Mrs. Tolando. She was one of the fourth grade teachers at The Ben Franklin School and everyone said she was really nice. But I didn't see why she couldn't be a teacher just because she was fat. Other teachers were fat. I remembered my mother being fat before Danny was born and touching her tummy to feel him kick.

Ruthie didn't say anything about having a new best friend, but she didn't say that we were still best friends either. She didn't say anything about the new family downstairs or how her brothers were or if she missed me. And she asked me to write back soon when she hadn't written back to me the whole year.

I hardly ever thought about New Haven anymore. It seemed so long ago that we had lived there. Whenever I asked my mother when we were going back to visit, she just said sometime. At first I had been really disappointed, but now it didn't seem so important. I mean, I still wanted to see the Greenbergs again, but if we didn't go back right away, I didn't mind as much as I used to.

chapter thirty-seven

When Mimi came over for the first time since she'd gotten sick, I hardly recognized her, she was so thin. Well, not really thin, but not fat either. She said she had lost twelve pounds. She was wearing a pair of her old shorts with a belt so they wouldn't fall down.

"My father bought me a new dress for school," she said. "Pretty soon he's going to buy me some other ones," she added. "My mother told him to wait a while, because she wants me to gain weight. She says I'm too skinny. But I don't think I am, do you?"

"You look really nice," I said. "I don't see why she wants you to."

"She says it's not healthy to be so thin. But I feel fine."

I asked her if she wanted to read. She said she did, so I opened *Mary Poppins* to where we had left off and we started in, taking turns. She was getting really good.

A few days later we walked to school together. She was wearing the new dress that her father had bought her and she looked really nice. When we got to school, the lines were already moving so nobody noticed us. If they had, they probably would have thought I was there with a brand-new kid. I wondered if even her teacher would recognize her.

Before she went into her classroom, I reminded her what she was supposed to do.

"Don't forget," I told her. "And let me know what she says."

Later on that morning, when it was snack time and the monitors were passing out milk and cookies, there was a knock on the door. It was Mrs. Russell, the principal. She came in and started talking to Miss Kerns in a low voice, so nobody could hear what she said. After she left, there was another knock. This time it was Mr. Fabian, the school janitor. He was carrying a desk.

"You can put it over there, Mr. Fabian," Miss Kerns said, pointing to a place in the third row next to Allie M. "I think it will be easier to move a few desks than to empty them all out."

While we all watched, Mr. Fabian went over and pushed Allie M's desk and Chester Peterson's desk out into the aisle and put the empty desk where Allie M's had been. Then he rearranged all of the other desks.

When he was done, he wiped his forehead with his red bandanna handkerchief.

"Thank you so much, Mr. Fabian," Miss Kerns said. "Boys and girls, please tell Mr. Fabian thank you."

"Thank you, Mr. Fabian," we all said in our best chorus voices.

After Mr. Fabian left, Miss Kerns told us another student would be joining our class.

"Most of you already know her," she said. "And I want all of you to make her feel welcome."

Everybody looked at each other and started whispering. Who could it be?

But I already knew.

chapter
thirty-eight

When Mimi came into the room with her teacher, at first no one recognized her. Then all of a sudden a few kids realized who she was and started whispering to the others. Nobody could believe how much she had changed.

Some of the kids knew she had had scarlet fever. There had been two other cases of it in our school, but none in our grade. So that explained why she wasn't fat anymore. But it didn't explain why was she going to be in the fourth grade after she had stayed back.

The third-grade teacher said hello. Except for me, she knew the whole class. She smiled a lot and didn't seem as strict as Miss Kerns. And she had her arm around Mimi's shoulder in the friendliest way, which wasn't like Miss Kerns at all.

"Boys and girls," Miss Kerns said. "Mrs. Dunn has something to tell you."

"I certainly do," Mrs. Dunn said. "It's a very special announcement. In fact, in all my years of teaching at Center School, I have never had occasion to make such an announcement before."

She looked down at Mimi. "You all know that Mimi has been repeating the third grade this year. She had missed a lot of school last year because of illness, and as a result her reading skills were not up to fourth-grade level. Well, this morning when Mimi returned to school after recovering from scarlet fever, she asked me to give her a reading test. And I am very pleased to announce that because of her splendid performance, as of today Mimi has been promoted to the fourth grade."

Mimi looked around the room. When she saw me, she gave a little smile. Without even thinking, I began to clap. And suddenly the whole class was clapping, too, and some of the boys were whistling and then Miss Kerns started clapping, too. Not to get us to stop but to join us.

You could see that Mimi couldn't believe what was happening. Her little smile got bigger and then bigger until she was grinning ear to ear. I had never seen anyone look so happy and proud.

Miss Kerns showed her where her new cubby was, and she put her lunchbox and sneakers in it. Then she took the rest of her things and put them in her new desk. Miss Kerns gave her the books we were using and asked Allie M, who sat next to her, to show her where we were in each of them. Then she called me up to her desk.

"I hear you're a good friend of Mimi's," she said.

I nodded.

"Mrs. Dunn said you've been helping Mimi with her reading."

I must have looked surprised that she knew, because she added, "Mimi told her. You must be a very good teacher."

"We've been reading *Mary Poppins* together," I said.

"Well, what I would like to ask you to do is help Mimi catch up here. I'll be working with her in our other subjects, but if you could spend some time each day reading with her, that would be a great help. And since you're such an excellent reader already, I think you might use part of your own reading period to work with Mimi. How does that sound?"

"It sounds okay," I said.

"Then that's our plan," Miss Kerns said. "You can think of yourself as my assistant. You might even decide to be a teacher, too, when you grow up."

"I'm going to be a writer," I said.

"Well, you might be both," Miss Kerns said. "Lots of writers have been teachers, too."

I never knew that. I had always thought you could only be one thing.

When it was reading period, Mimi and I used the little

corner table where the fish tank was. Our reading book was called *The Road to Reading.* Each chapter was a new story on the road and most of them were pretty boring. Mimi's chapter was at the very beginning so it was easy. It was about a girl who got lost in the woods one day and met a fox that could talk and pretended to be her friend but really wanted to trick her.

Mimi was able to read it without much help so I started thinking about other things. Mostly Dan. I wished he lived near me so we could see each other after school, but he didn't. He lived in exactly the opposite direction from where I did, near Allie M's house. She said his family was on relief. That meant that they didn't have enough money to buy food, so someone had to give it to them. It was because of the Depression.

Allie M told me Dan had a paper route so he could earn money to help his family. He had to get up at five o'clock every morning so he could deliver the newspapers before school. In the wintertime it was still dark at five o'clock. I couldn't imagine getting up that early and going out in the dark all by myself. It was really brave. It made me like him even more.

chapter thirty-nine

After school Mimi and I walked home together. She still couldn't believe what had happened.

"And it's all because of you, Allie," she said, her eyes filling with tears. "If it hadn't been for you, I'd still be in the third grade."

By now I knew that Mimi cried when she was sad and when she was happy, both. These were happy tears.

"But you were the one who worked so hard," I said, secretly pleased that she gave me so much credit. "Of course *Mary Poppins* had a lot to do with it, too."

"It's such a wonderful book!" Mimi said. "I never want it to end!"

"When it does, you can just go back and read it all over again," I told her. "That's what I do."

When we got home, I told her I'd come get her in the morning before school. I knew she had hoped I would ask her over to play. But I didn't. I really wanted to see Martha by myself that afternoon. I had something important to ask her.

While I had my milk and graham crackers, I told my mother and Danny about Mimi's promotion and how I was now Miss Kerns's assistant. My mother said she was really proud of me. And Danny said he would draw a picture of Mary Poppins for Mimi and write "congratulations" on it.

While I was up in my room changing my clothes, I heard Martha calling for me.

She was waiting on the back porch. I told her about what had happened in school.

"That's really great," she said. She was really impressed. "What should we do this afternoon?"

I took a deep breath. "I saw Cynthia at your house yesterday."

Martha looked embarrassed. Finally she said, "She was only there for a little while."

"So she's allowed to come over again?"

Martha nodded.

I swallowed hard. "Is she your best friend now?"

Martha didn't answer.

"She is, isn't she?"

"It's just that I see her in school every day. And I've known her a lot longer."

"So we're not best friends anymore," I said. "Even at home."

"Don't be mad," Martha said. "We can still be really good friends."

"No, we can't."

"Why not?"

"Because it isn't fair. Once you're best friends with somebody, you shouldn't just all of a sudden be best friends with somebody else."

"That's exactly what Cynthia said," Martha said. "She said that's what I did when I decided to be best friends with you. She said she was my best friend first."

I knew that was true. But I felt all mixed up. If Cynthia was right, then you had to have one best friend for your whole life and you could never change. That meant I was still best friends with Ruthie, which I wasn't. But maybe if you moved away, that was different. You couldn't keep being best friends with somebody you never even saw.

"Don't be mad," Martha said. "I still like you a lot."

But liking someone a lot wasn't the same as liking her best of all.

chapter forty

It turned out that hardly anything changed between Martha and me except when Cynthia came over. The rest of the time we played together the way we always had, only now most days Mimi joined us. She still thought Martha and I were best friends. Sometimes I still thought so, too, until I remembered.

Martha acted as if nothing had ever happened. But we didn't call each other by our secret names anymore. And she never mentioned Cynthia, not once. It was as if when we were together we both pretended she didn't exist.

When Martha was with Cynthia, Mimi and I played by ourselves. A few times Allie M came over and then the three of us played together. But even though neither Martha nor I ever said anything, each time that Allie M visited me, Martha stayed home, even if Cynthia wasn't there. It was as if she wanted to pretend that Allie M didn't exist either.

Something else happened, too, something really important.

Mr. and Mrs. Minnick weren't going to get divorced. And Mr. Minnick wasn't a bookie anymore. He had gotten a new job. Now he was a salesman, just like my father. Only he didn't sell insurance like my father did, he sold men's clothes at C.O. Martin's, the biggest store in Stamford.

Sometimes he brought Mimi new clothes from C.O. Martin's. Once he even brought me a new blouse. It was just like one he had gotten for Mimi, only hers was yellow and mine was pink. He said it was a thank-you present because I was responsible for Mimi's promotion.

And Mrs. Minnick had gotten nicer. But she still liked to say sarcastic things sometimes and nag Mimi about her eating. Only now it was because Mimi didn't eat a lot, not because she did. She was always telling us to have another cookie or more soda.

By now we had finished *Mary Poppins* and had started in on *Heidi*. We didn't read over the phone anymore, we just read chapters separately and talked about them when we were together. Of course I had already read *Heidi* four or five times but I still loved it.

But *Mary Poppins* was still Mimi's favorite. She read it over and over again until she practically knew it by heart. And she was always saying "Mary Poppins would really like this," and "Mary Poppins wouldn't do that," as if Mary Poppins was a real person.

And then the strangest thing happened.

One afternoon Mimi and I were playing Monopoly in my room when she said she wanted to tell me something. She said that after her parents had told her that they weren't going to get a divorce, she had asked when her father was going to move back. At that time it was still April, just a little while after Mimi had gotten over being sick. And they had said they didn't know, that they were talking to someone called a social worker about how to get along better together and not have fights and that the social worker would tell them when she thought they were ready to live together again. And every time Mimi asked them about it, she got the same answer. And now a whole month had gone by and her father still hadn't come home.

Then the night before, she told me, she had gotten this picture in her mind. It wasn't a dream, she said, because even though she was in bed she wasn't sleeping and her eyes were wide open. It was more like a play she was watching but inside her head. Someone was walking down the street toward her. As the person got nearer, she saw that it was Mary Poppins. Her cheeks were bright red and she was wearing her funny little hat. Then all of a sudden she turned and called to somebody behind her, "Good evening, Mr. Minnick! Only two more weeks and you'll be coming home."

"That's weird," I said. "Do you really believe it?"

"Of course I do," she said. "Mary Poppins said so."

"Are you sure your mother didn't just tell you and you forgot?"

"Come on over to my house," Mimi said. "I'll prove she didn't."

We found Mrs. Minnick at the kitchen table as usual, listening to the radio and drinking orange soda.

"Do you know when Daddy's coming home?" Mimi asked her.

"Shhh!" Mrs. Minnick said. "Don't interrupt my program."

It was *Ma Perkins*. My mother liked *Ma Perkins*, too.

"I just want to know when Daddy's coming back," Mimi repeated in a loud whisper.

"How many times do I have to tell you that we don't know yet!" Mrs. Minnick said crossly.

Mimi gave me a triumphant look. "You see?" she said. "Now promise me you won't tell anybody."

I crossed my heart. "But it still doesn't prove anything," I said. "He might come home on another day."

"He's coming home in two weeks," Mimi insisted. "On May twenty-fifth. Mary Poppins said so."

After I went home, I kept thinking about what she had

said. In the end I decided that she had just read *Mary Poppins* too many times and gotten sort of weird herself. Nobody could predict the future. But I put a circle around May 25 on my calendar and then I got my good-luck aggie from under my mattress and rubbed it hard, just in case.

chapter forty-one

A little while later I heard Martha calling for me. I went downstairs and found her waiting for me on our back porch. She looked really worried.

"I have something to ask you," she said. "Only you've got to promise not to tell anybody."

I said I would.

"I mean really promise," she said.

I crossed my heart and hoped to die.

"It's about Cynthia," she said.

I felt a little shiver. It was the first time she had mentioned Cynthia since that time she had told me they were best friends again.

"Remember when Cynthia called you a cheater that time?" she asked.

I nodded. How could I ever forget it?

"Well, Cynthia's the real cheater," Martha whispered. "A really bad one. And nobody knows about it but me."

She told me that in school that day they had had a spelling test. Sister Mary Louise had dictated a list of words and they were supposed to write them down. They were words from last night's homework. And Martha had noticed that Cynthia kept pushing back the cuff on her sleeve and looking down at her wrist. And then she had seen that there was writing on Cynthia's arm, underneath her blouse.

"Our desks are in the last row, so there's no one in back of us," Martha said. "I was the only one who could see what she was doing."

"Are you going to tell?" I asked.

"I don't know," Martha said. "I don't want to be a tattletale."

I knew you shouldn't tattle, but still it wasn't fair for Cynthia to cheat like that. And I had to admit I wouldn't mind Cynthia getting into trouble after what she had done to me and for making Martha be her best friend again.

"Did you tell Cynthia you saw her?"

Martha shook her head. "I was afraid to. You know how she can be when she doesn't like you."

I knew exactly what she meant.

"And then, right after the test, she asked to be excused to go to the girls' room."

"To wash it off?" I asked.

"I guess so. So there was no proof. But I saw her do it."

"Maybe you should ask your mother what to do," I said.

"But what if she makes me tell Sister? If Cynthia finds out, she'll never speak to me again."

I didn't think that would be so awful, but of course I couldn't tell Martha that. "Well, you could just forget it," I said.

"Do you think so?" Martha asked hopefully. "Do you think that would be all right?"

I knew it wasn't right but I knew how Martha felt. But something else was bothering me, something I couldn't quite figure out.

After Martha went home, I kept thinking about what she had told me. And suddenly I knew what else was wrong. It was that she still wanted to be best friends with someone like Cynthia, someone who could be so nasty and who cheated, besides. And then I wondered something else. I wondered why I still wanted to be best friends with someone who still wanted to be best friends with someone like Cynthia.

chapter
forty-two

"Guess what day it is?" Mimi asked me one afternoon when we were walking home from school.

"It's Tuesday," I said. "So what?"

"No, the date," Mimi said. "Guess what date it is?"

"I don't know."

"It's *May twenty-fifth.*"

May 25! I had forgotten all about it!

"The day my father's coming home!"

I looked across the street but Mr. Minnick's car wasn't there. Mimi saw what I was thinking. "It's only four o'clock," she said. "He has until midnight."

"He won't come home at midnight," I said.

"I didn't say he would. But he still has eight hours. He's probably still working."

"Well, I hope you're right," I said.

"Of course I'm right," Mimi said. "Mary Poppins said so."

After Mimi went home, I started to do my homework. I had a lot of it, but I had a hard time concentrating. Every few minutes I would look out the window to see if Mr. Minnick's car was there, but it never was. When it was time for supper, I looked one last time but it still wasn't there. Poor Mimi. She would be so disappointed if Mary Poppins was wrong. But how could a make-believe person in a book know what was going to happen in the future? The whole thing was crazy.

While we were eating, the telephone rang. My mother got up to answer it.

"Oh, hello, Mimi," she said. "No, I'm afraid Allie is eating her supper now. I'll have her call you later."

I leaped up and grabbed the phone out of my mother's hand.

"Mimi?" I said. "Mimi, I'm here. Did he . . . ?"

For a minute there was silence, and then Mimi spoke in a trembling voice and I knew she was crying.

"He's home, Allie! My father's come home!"

Suddenly I felt goose bumps all over.

"Well, what was that about?" my mother asked after I hung up the phone.

I told them the whole story, about Mimi's sort-of-dream and Mary Poppins's prediction. And then I went and got my calendar to show them.

"Well, that is uncanny," my father said, looking really puzzled. "Are you sure her mother didn't tell her?"

I repeated that I had been there when Mrs. Minnick had said she didn't know when Mr. Minnick was coming home.

"What's uncanny?" I asked.

"It's when something strange happens and can't be explained logically," my father said.

"It's probably just a coincidence," my mother said. "But it is odd, isn't it?"

I didn't say anything. But somehow I didn't think it was a coincidence at all. I thought it was uncanny.

chapter

forty-three

It was the last day of school. Everybody was staying for lunch and we were going to have a picnic out on the playground. Some of the mothers were bringing the food. My mother was one of them. Mrs. Minnick was, too. She had baked chocolate chip cookies.

When Mimi called for me that morning, she was all dressed up.

"How pretty you look, Mimi," my mother said. "Is that a new dress?"

Mimi blushed. She still wasn't used to people giving her compliments.

"My father bought it," she said.

"How is your father?" my mother asked. "Does he like his new job?"

Mimi nodded. "And he gets a discount on everything he buys in the store. Even ladies' clothes. He bought my mother a new dress, too."

"That's wonderful," my mother said.

"We better go," I said. I couldn't wait to talk to Mimi about our plan.

As soon as we left, I asked her what time her father was coming to school. She said just before lunch.

"He'll come to our door and knock three times. That's the signal. Then we'll go out and get her."

No one knew about our secret plan except Allie M and Miss Kerns and Mr. Minnick. And of course Mr. Sherwood. Not even our mothers or my father knew.

"Do you have the grass?" she asked me.

"I picked it as soon as I got up this morning," I said. "It's in my lunch box."

She laughed. "Well, it *is* a lunch! Only not for you."

All morning long Allie M and Mimi and I kept looking over at each other. I could hardly concentrate on anything. At snack time Allie M was the milk monitor. When she gave me my milk, she whispered, "I've got the ribbon in my pocket."

All of a sudden I remembered that I had something in my pocket, too. That morning I had been looking at my aggie when my mother called me for breakfast and I had stuck it in my pocket instead of putting it back under my mattress. I looked over at Dan, wondering what he would think if he knew.

Reading period had never gone by so slowly. Mimi was a Crow now, and I didn't have to help her anymore. Now I was helping Betsy Richardson, who was a Chickadee. She was the only Chickadee left. The other two had flown up to the Blue Jays.

When the clock reached 11:29, I held my breath. Then, just as the big hand jumped to 30, there were three loud knocks on the door. Everyone looked up. Miss Kerns nodded her head at me. I grabbed my lunch box and ran to the door with Allie M and Mimi following. I opened it a little bit, just enough to let us slip through into the hall.

And there she was. Mr. Minnick was holding her on a leash like a dog. Allie M tied the pink ribbon around her neck in a great big bow. I gave her a handful of grass. Her soft tongue licked my fingers clean.

We took the leash from Mr. Minnick and led her into the classroom. When we came in, the whole class burst out laughing and Miss Kerns joined in. They clapped and whistled and stamped their feet on the floor. I waited until everyone had quieted down. Then I said in a loud voice:

"Rule Number 7 — No lambs at school except with permission of the teacher."

I turned to Miss Kerns and she started to laugh again. It made her look like a different person.

"When I wrote Rule 7, I must admit that I never thought that anyone would actually do it," she said, still laughing. "It just seemed like a funny idea. But then when Allie S and

Allie M and Mimi took me at my word and actually asked for permission, of course I couldn't say no."

The whole class lined up, with Allie M and Mimi and me and the lamb, whose name was Dorabelle, leading the way. It was like a parade. As we marched down the hall, we sang "Mary Had a Little Lamb," and one by one all the doors opened to see what was going on.

As soon as they saw Dorabelle, kids came running out into the corridor, reaching out to pat her as she went by. She looked so cute prancing along with the big pink ribbon tied around her neck. Mr. Minnick was standing outside the entrance with a camera, and as we came out the front door, he had us stop so he could take our picture. Then we led Dorabelle out to the playground.

The mothers had set up a long table on the girls' side. It was covered with a red-and-white checkered tablecloth and there were plates with piles of sandwiches and cookies and pitchers of lemonade. When they saw us coming, they looked at each other in amazement. Danny, who was there with our mother, started jumping up and down.

"It's Dorabelle!" he yelled. "It's Dorabelle from Mr. Sherwood's farm!"

Mrs. Minnick was standing next to my mother. As we walked over to them, Mimi whispered that her mother was wearing the new dress her father had bought her from C.O. Martin's.

"Doesn't she look pretty?" Mimi asked.

She really did. She was wearing lipstick and her hair was all waved, and even though she was fat, you didn't notice it as much in her new dress. Besides, as I looked around the table at all the mothers, I saw that there were other fat ones, too, some even as fat as Mrs. Minnick. I saw Dan next to one of them. When he saw me looking at him, he took her hand and led her over to me.

"Momma, this is Allie S," he said.

Dan's mother put out her hand and I shook it. It was chapped and rough-feeling, not smooth and soft like my mother's hands.

"Danny's told me about you," Mrs. Borelli said. She had the nicest smile. "He told me how you helped Mimi with her reading so she could be promoted."

I felt myself blushing. "Well, Dan helps you," I blurted out. "With his paper route."

As soon as I said it, I felt awful. Would it embarrass Dan to know that I knew about his paper route? Would he think that meant I knew he was poor and that they were on relief?

But Mrs. Borelli just patted Dan's head and smiled some more. "He's a wonderful boy," she said. "I don't know what I'd do without him. Of course, sometimes I don't know what to do *with* him, either."

Now Dan started to blush, too. We both stood there, looking at each other, not saying anything.

"I hope you'll come over and visit us sometime," Mrs. Borelli said. "Dan says you have a little brother. Danny has one, too. Maybe they could play together."

"Joey," Dan said. "He's five."

"So is Danny," I said.

"So you have a Danny, too," Mrs. Borelli said.

"They call me Danny at home," Dan mumbled.

All of a sudden I realized that Mrs. Borelli reminded me of Mrs. Greenberg. Both of them were warm and funny and friendly. Mrs. Borelli even looked a little like Mrs. Greenberg with her dark curly hair and the crinkles around her eyes.

By now everybody was lining up for lunch. I said good-bye to Mrs. Borelli and Dan and went to find Mimi. She was standing in line with her father and Dorabelle.

"Well, we pulled it off!" Mr. Minnick said. He looked at his wristwatch. "It's about time for me to go back to work. Do you girls want to help me with Dorabelle?"

We led Dorabelle over to Mr. Minnick's car. As soon as he got in and offered her a piece of sandwich, she jumped right in beside him.

We watched them drive off together. Then we got our lunch and sat down on a bench.

"That was fun," I said. "Your father was really nice to bring Dorabelle."

Mimi smiled. "He's nice almost all the time now. So is my mother. They hardly ever even have fights anymore. Just once in a while. And do you know something else?"

I shook my head.

"It's because of me that my father came back to live with us. He said so." She got her happy crybaby look. "He told me that when I had scarlet fever and they were so worried that I might die, that's when he and my mother decided that if . . . that when I got better he would come home again."

"That's wonderful," I said. I looked over at Allie M, who was sitting with Dan and his mother. I put my hand in my pocket and rubbed my aggie. I wished that Allie M's father would come back home, too.

chapter forty-four

The next day Mimi and I decided to have a picnic down in the field. When Danny said he wanted to come with us, Mimi said no even before I did, which really surprised me.

"Not today, Danny," she told him. "Allie and I want to be by ourselves now. But you can play with us this afternoon."

Danny started to pout, but Mimi said we'd have a big surprise for him later on.

As we walked down the hill, I said I'd never heard her say no to Danny before.

"Well, today is special," Mimi said. "The surprise is for you, too, and I don't want anyone else to be there when I show it to you."

Now I really was curious. I begged her to tell me what it was but she wouldn't.

When we got to the field, we started looking around for a good place to have our picnic, one without any cow plops.

"Oh, look!" Mimi said suddenly. She came over and handed me something. It was a four-leaf clover.

"Wow!" I said, cradling it in the palm of my hand. I had never in my whole life found a four-leaf clover.

"I can find them whenever I want to," Mimi said. "Almost anywhere."

She knelt down and started peering at the ground. In just a few seconds she had found another one. I couldn't believe it.

After we had our picnic, Mimi said it was time.

"Time for what?" I asked.

"For the surprise," she said.

We walked back up the hill and into her backyard.

"Wait a minute," she said.

She went into her house and came out again with two little baskets.

"Follow me." She led me around to behind her garage. I had never been there before. It was all overgrown with vines and tangles. We climbed up a rock and over a low wall.

"This isn't our yard anymore," Mimi whispered. "We've got to be very quiet."

"Who lives here?" I whispered back.

"Mrs. Hurlburt. She's an old lady and she never comes outside, but we still have to be careful. We're trespassing on her property."

We were at the back of a long narrow yard. There were

tall bushes along the back of the house that hid the windows and the grass wasn't mowed. It was really spooky.

Mimi bent over and began to look. I wondered if she was looking for more four-leaf clovers. Then suddenly she let out a squeal and held out her hand. In it was a teeny tiny little red ball. It was a strawberry!

"Go ahead, eat it!" Mimi said.

I put it in my mouth and slowly rolled it around on my tongue. It was yummy, like a regular strawberry and yet different, sweet and not sweet at the same time. I had never tasted anything quite like it.

We crouched down and started looking for more of them. They were so small you could hardly see them, hidden under their little scalloped leaves and the tall grass. I tried to save some in my basket, but I kept popping them into my mouth almost as fast as I picked them.

"How did you discover them?" I asked Mimi.

"One day when I was in first grade I was exploring," she said. "I was looking for four-leaf clovers and I thought maybe there would be some over in Mrs. Hurlburt's yard. So I climbed over the wall and snuck in. I didn't find any clovers but I found the strawberries. And every June since then I've gone back to pick them. But I haven't ever told anybody about them until you."

Suddenly I remembered that day when I had started to

read *Mary Poppins* to her over the telephone and had told her about how disappointed I had been when there weren't any strawberries on Strawberry Hill.

"You knew then, didn't you?" I asked.

"Of course."

"Then why didn't you tell me?"

"I almost did," she said. "But then I decided it would be more fun to surprise you in the spring, when the strawberries were really here."

She explained that each year was different. It depended on how much sun and rain there had been. Sometimes there weren't any until the end of June but this year she had found the first ones a few days before school was over.

"Last year you didn't move here until after they were gone," she told me.

As we talked, we kept picking them. They really were good, even though they were so tiny. Much better than store ones.

"Don't eat them all," Mimi said. "I promised to save some for Danny."

"But then they won't be a secret anymore," I said.

"That's okay. I only kept them a secret because I didn't have anybody I wanted to tell about them."

After we had picked enough strawberries to fill one of the little baskets, we sat down to rest on the wall behind Mimi's garage. I didn't say anything. Only it wasn't because I didn't have anything to say, it was because I was thinking what words to use to say what I wanted to.

"Mimi?" Her name came out as a little squeak.

She turned to look at me. "What?"

"Would you like to be best friends with me?"

Her eyes widened. She looked as if she couldn't believe what I had said. "Me?" she said. "You want to be best friends with me?"

I nodded. "I've been thinking about it for a long time. Do you want to?"

She bit her lip. "What about Martha?"

"Martha used to be my best friend," I said. "But when she went back to Cynthia, she wasn't anymore."

"So you're just asking me because you can't have Martha," Mimi said in a flat voice.

I shook my head. "That's not it. Even if I could be best friends with her again, I wouldn't. I'd rather be best friends with you."

Mimi looked doubtful. "Why?"

"Because I really like you," I said. Then I remembered what Danny had said about her. "And because you're so interesting."

In two weeks it would be my birthday. We had lived here almost a whole year. And during that year I had had three best friends, Ruthie, Martha, and now Mimi. I remembered feeling so awful when Martha went back to Cynthia, but now I didn't care anymore. We were still friends, but not best friends. My new best friend was much more interesting. She had predicted when her father was coming home and she could find four-leaf clovers and she had discovered that there really were strawberries on Strawberry Hill. She might even have magical powers like Mary Poppins.

And then I remembered how when we still lived in New Haven, I had pictured the wall with the white gate at the bottom of the hill. And how I had gotten the measles just when I needed to. And about my free stick. And about how I had helped Mimi to get promoted. And about my good-luck aggie and how I had rubbed it to help Mr. Minnick come home. And best of everything, how Strawberry Hill did have strawberries after all, and they were even better than I had imagined.

It was all really uncanny. Maybe I had some magical powers, too.

Or maybe it was Strawberry Hill that was magic.

The End

Don't miss these great picture books
by Mary Ann Hoberman:

All Kinds of Families!

The Eensy-Weensy Spider

I Know an Old Lady Who Swallowed a Fly

The Lady with the Alligator Purse

Mary Had a Little Lamb

Miss Mary Mack

Mrs. O'Leary's Cow

My Song Is Beautiful

One of Each

You Read to Me, I'll Read to You: Very Short Fairy Tales to Read Together

You Read to Me, I'll Read to You: Very Short Mother Goose Tales to Read Together

You Read to Me, I'll Read to You: Very Short Scary Tales to Read Together

You Read to Me, I'll Read to You: Very Short Stories to Read Together